Also by R.A. Salvatore

The Legend of Drizzt®

Homeland

Exile

Sojourn

The Crystal Shard

Streams of Silver

The Halfling's Gem

The Legacy

Starless Night

Siege of Darkness

Passage to Dawn

The Silent Blade

The Spine of the World

Sea of Swords

Also by R.A. & Geno Salvatore

The Stowaway
Stone of Tymora, Book I

STONE OF TYMORA BOOK II

THE SHADOWMASK

R.A. SALVATORE
& GENO

STONE OF TYMORA   BOOK II

THE SHADOWMASK

R.A. SALVATORE
& GENO

MIRRORSTONE

The Shadowmask

Published by Wizards of the Coast LLC

MIRRORSTONE, FORGOTTEN REALMS, DUNGEONS & DRAGONS, WIZARDS OF THE COAST, their respective logos and LEGEND OF DRIZZT are trademarks of Wizards of the Coast LLC in the U.S.A. and other countries.

Printed in the U.S.A.

Cover art by Todd Lockwood
Map by Robert Lazzaretti
First Printing: November 2009

9 8 7 6 5 4 3 2 1

ISBN: 978-0-7869-5147-5
620- 24057720-001-EN

Library of Congress Cataloging-in-Publication Data
Salvatore, R. A., 1959-
The shadowmask / R.A. & Geno Salvatore.
   p. cm. -- (Stone of Tymora ; bk. 2)
"Mirrorstone."
Summary: Armed with his late mentor's cloak and magical sword, Maimon sets out on a dangerous and adventurous journey determined to find the stolen stone of Tymora and avenge the death of his mentor while eluding the evil demon Asbeel, who is also searching for the precious stone.
   ISBN 978-0-7869-5147-5
[1. Orphans--Fiction. 2. Adventure and adventurers--Fiction. 3. Fantasy.]
I. Salvatore, Geno. II. Title.
PZ7.S15535Sh 2009
[Fic]--dc22

                                                                    2009023094

U.S., CANADA,   EUROPEAN HEADQUARTERS
ASIA, PACIFIC, & LATIN AMERICA   Hasbro UK Ltd
Wizards of the Coast LLC   Caswell Way
P.O. Box 707   Newport, Gwent NP9 0YH
Renton, WA 98057-0707   GREAT BRITAIN
+1-800-324-6496
            Please keep this address for your records.
          Visit our Web site at www.mirrorstonebooks.com

09 10 11 12 13 14 15   QW-FF

For all the teachers who helped shape my life.

—G.S.

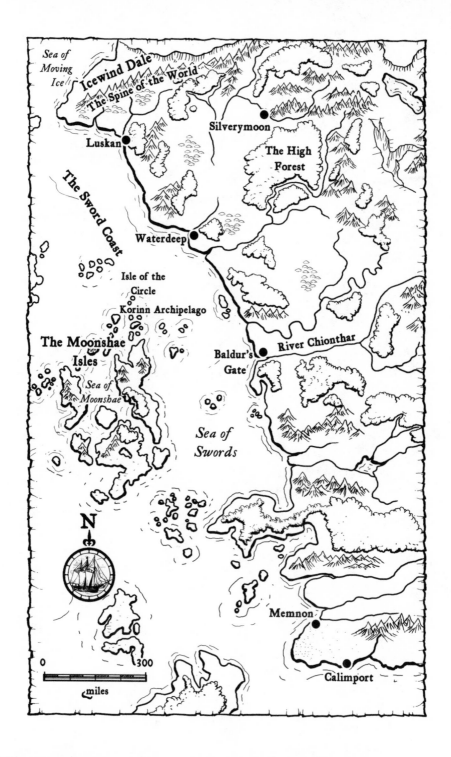

Part One

THE SHADOWMASK

Light poured into the tiny, dirty chamber, waking me from my sleep. I looked up and shaded my eyes. Sunlight shone directly in through the short passage that led to the beach outside. But I couldn't tell if it was morning or evening, if we faced west or east.

At that moment, it hardly seemed to matter. A tall man stood in the doorway, leaning slightly to his right, awkward on his wooden peg leg. With a shuffle and a clomp, he stepped into the room. The door swung shut behind him, snuffing out all the light save what little came in through the crack at the bottom of the portal.

"Ye got more story to be telling me, or is this the day I be killing ye?" he asked gruffly. He placed something between his knees—a torch, I guessed. I heard the scrape of flint across tinder as he tried to light the thing.

"You're planning to kill me when I finish the story?" I asked.

"Yar, probably so. The boys don't like holding prisoners fer too long, seeing as it means we can't be out sailing."

"Out plundering and murdering, you mean."

"Call it what ye will," he said with a chuckle.

"If you're going to kill me anyway, why should I continue the story at all?"

The pirate laughed. "Ye've seen men die before, whelp. Ye know what tha's like. Ask any o' them what they'd've done fer one more day! I be sure telling an old salt like me a bit o' story wouldn't be too much trouble."

Steel clicked against flint once more, and a few sparks flew out, revealing the old pirate's face and the horrible gold-toothed grin splayed across it. But the sparks didn't take on the torch, and again he was in shadow.

"This coming from a man who wouldn't know," I said. "You've never cared about death, not your own nor anyone else's."

"Strong words, whelp," he snarled. "But ye're off yer mark. I had me day o' dying once, and I were bargaining much as I could, with any who'd listen. And only by the grace o' the gods did I live."

Again sparks flew as steel struck flint. The pirate's smile was gone, his face flat in the eerie light. But again the torch did not light.

"And I see you've paid the debt you promised them," I said sarcastically.

"That I have, that I have!" the pirate replied. "I swore I'd live each and ev'ry day as if it were my last. And I ain't missed one yet. Now, I'm offering ye a chance, boy. Either this day is yer last, or ye tell me the next part o' yer story."

A third time flint and steel struck and sparks flew. Finally the oil-soaked rag of the torch caught a spark and lit.

CHAPTER ONE

"Where is the stone?" the raspy voice whispered from above me.

I scrambled back on all fours. Asbeel's boot paced me. I felt the dull impact in my midsection, but I hardly noticed the pain through the mental fog that clouded my memory. Where had the stone gone?

"Where is it?" Asbeel's boot lashed out again.

A black mask of carved obsidian, a shadow beneath the hood of a flowing black robe, leered at me from my mind's eye. She spoke, her voice so soft, so gentle. Her voice . . . I had heard it only once, yet it felt so familiar.

The boot leaped at me again, aiming for my head. I brought my arms up, absorbing the brunt of the blow, but the force was still enough to send me into a roll. The wall of the narrow alley met me halfway through the tumble, and the impact knocked the breath from my body.

I turned my gaze upward, following the arc of the muscled leg hidden beneath black breeches; to a leather vest, and the red-tinted arms crossed in front of the chest; to the leering face, angular and bald, its red eyes glowing with angry fire. And beside the creature's head, the hilt of a sword, a horrible creation of jagged metal—an evil blade to match the demon's evil soul.

The demon. Asbeel. He had pursued me across the length of the Sword Coast. His sword. That same blade had felled my mentor Perrault.

Time moved more slowly, all sensations becoming more distinct: the loose sand of the alley; the rough stone of the wall behind me, unfinished and easy to climb; the sky above, lightening with the sunrise, taking away the demon's advantage of darkness. Without realizing I had moved at all, I found my hand resting on the hilt of my own weapon, the stiletto Perrault had once wielded. The fog lifted from my mind; my vision was suddenly remarkably clear.

Asbeel spoke again. "Where is the—"

"I do not have it." My voice did not crack, did not waver at all. "And neither shall you."

I jumped to my feet, and my hand snapped forward, bringing the narrow dagger to bear in front of me. The momentum of my sudden motion rolled down the blade, lengthening the weapon into a fine saber. I fell into a lunge as the sword tip leaped for Asbeel's black heart.

But Asbeel simply stepped backward.

I teetered at full extension, my trailing foot against the wall, the tip of my sword a foot from Asbeel. My moment of vengeance turned to defeat; my elation turned to fear. My mind raced as I tried to recall the swordfights I'd read about or seen. My feet scrambled to form an L shape, and I struggled to hold the sword vertically in front of me.

Asbeel reached up to his shoulder. Somehow he found a handle to grip among the sharp, twisting spikes on his sword. The wickedly serrated, curved blade slowly rose from behind him. As soon as its tip cleared its sheath, the whole blade burst into red flame. Still moving slowly, deliberately, Asbeel gripped the hilt in both hands and tapped the dull edge of the blade to his forehead in a mock salute.

The blade's fire danced wildly, mesmerizing, tantalizing, beautiful and horrible all at once. My heartbeat drummed in my ears.

With a snarl, the demon leaped forward. He swung his sword in a wide arc. The fire seemed to hang in the air behind the curved blade.

But I was ready. I brought my sword to bear against his in a textbook-perfect parry.

Or so I thought.

The sheer force of the demon's blow nearly ripped my saber from my hand. I tried to roll with the momentum of the strike, to absorb some of its power. I could not hold my footing, and my skull cracked hard against the ground.

I felt warmth on the back of my head, a trickle of blood. A wave of dizziness washed over me. I could not catch my breath. The demon would be upon me before I could right myself.

But the killing blow did not fall.

After what seemed an eternity, the world stopped spinning. I rose unsteadily and turned to face Asbeel.

The demon had not moved. He matched my stare, but in his eyes I saw not rage, only amusement. Again he tapped his sword to his forehead, saluting me, mocking me.

"You wear his clothes, boy," said the demon. "But you do not honor him with your fighting."

"You know nothing of honor," I growled.

"I know your mentor would be ashamed to see you fight so wretchedly."

"The only thing he wouldn't like," I said calmly, "is that I bothered to talk to you." I lunged forward suddenly. Steel clashed against black iron, but my blade cut nothing but air.

I retracted my arm quickly and struck again. I did not fully commit myself, but shortened my lunge. When the demon brought his blade across to parry, I rolled my wrist, twisted my saber around the demon's sword, and pushed my leading leg forward, extending my arm to its full length. My sword's tip reached out for Asbeel's chest, stretching, reaching. . . .

Asbeel's empty hand shot across his chest and grabbed my sword by the blade. My sword slipped a bit. Its perfect edge drew a line of blood across the demon's hand, but he did not seem to notice.

"You do not deserve that sword, boy," he said with a wicked laugh. "So I shall take it from you."

I gritted my teeth and yanked at the sword. I felt its edge dig in to the demon's flesh, but he only tightened his grip in response. The sword would move no further.

I wanted to release the sword, to leap at Asbeel's smug face, to punch him, kick him, whatever I could do to fight back. But the idea of my sword—Perrault's sword—in that beast's possession, even for a moment, made me ill. How many times had I seen Perrault use that sword—for show more often than for combat— twirling it about expertly, mixing the straight lines of lunges with dazzling curving strikes, the blade's magical blue flame trailing behind it.

Blue flame . . .

A brilliant line of cerulean fire pierced the dark air, engulfing my sword from crosspiece to tip—and Asbeel's clawed hand with it.

Asbeel's unearthly scream cut the stillness of the dawn. The alley became a clutter of motion as rats and bats fled its shadows. I wanted nothing more than to turn and follow them. But I stood my ground.

Asbeel's face twisted in pain. After a long moment, he released the sword, and I stumbled back.

For the first time, I had the upper hand against the beast. I took a step toward him, then another. I would kill Asbeel with the sword of my fallen mentor. I was worthy of the weapon.

I lunged ahead one final time, lunged right past the demon's outstretched arms, lunged right at his black heart.

But as my sword reached the demon, he disappeared.

Asbeel's fist clubbed the back of my head. I tumbled forward, away from him, yet somehow I landed right at his feet. He kicked at me several times. At last I managed to scramble away.

I pulled myself up to all fours and took an awkward half-running, half-leaping step, propelling me over the short stack of crates separating the alley from the market square.

But he was already there as I landed. He stood over me, his sword upraised.

"Stop."

The word was whispered, but its effect was immediate. The demon and I turned in unison to face a hooded figure emerging from the shadows across the square.

She wore a black robe, her cowl pulled low, her face hidden in shadow. No, not shadow, but a shadow-mask, black as night and carved into an expressionless human face. A cold chill ran down my spine. It was the same woman, the same creature, who had assaulted me the previous night, the same being who had stolen from me that which was most precious.

"Child, come to me," the woman said, beckoning. I took the first steps to oblige, relieved to step away from the demon and be rescued from the impossible fight. But I stopped after a few short paces.

The demon cackled behind me. "You call to him now, do you? Twice you abandon him, yet now you call to him?"

"Ignore him," she said sweetly. "Come to me."

Every instinct I possessed cried out that I should go to her. But somewhere in my rational mind I remembered her words from the previous night, and how I had fallen asleep against my will. Was there magic in the words she uttered?

How else could she have stopped Asbeel so completely, just as he was readying a killing blow? Or was she in league with the demon, tricking me into letting my guard down so he could kill me with ease? What more could she want from me, given that she had the stone?

I flexed the fingers of my left hand instinctively, and a slight tingle traced its way from my fingertips to my heart, to the hollow of my chest where the stone had once rested in its leather pouch.

I yearned to be reunited with that stone, wanting it back with every fiber of my being. It had been my curse. Before I returned to Memnon, I had intended to be rid of it. It was powerful, to be sure, and the luck it provided had saved my skin more than once. But its power was not the reason I craved its return. It was my destiny, my legacy, the only thing that remained of my family. And yet the masked woman had the stone. She had stolen it from me, and it belonged to me, not to her.

I raised the sword, still burning a fiery blue. "Where is it?" I asked her. "Where is the stone?"

Again Asbeel cackled. "Yes, do tell," he said sarcastically.

"Begone, wretch!" Gone was the woman's whisper, replaced by a roar as loud as a riled bear's. A group of ravens lifted off from the rooftop above me, their wings shining in the light of the new dawn.

I heard a faint popping sound. When I turned, Asbeel had disappeared.

I dropped to a crouch and brought my sword above me. I looked up, scanning the rooftops for the demon. I was certain he would be swooping in to attack me at any moment. But the first rays of sun broke over the horizon, illuminating the sky, and no dark shadows floated there.

Asbeel was simply gone.

I glanced back at the cloaked woman just in time to see her fade into the shadows of the market's eastern edge.

"Wait!"

Chapter Two

I flew through the winding, narrow streets of Memnon, following the slightest flicker of darkness. The masked woman's black cloak seemed always but a few yards in front of me, just on the edge of my vision. Every turn I took, every new street I entered, there she was, just rounding the next bend.

I had not come to Memnon looking for the woman. I had entered the city to save *Sea Sprite* and her crew—the crew I had put in danger. I had planned to pass through Memnon on my way to some place where I could safely be rid of the stone without fear that it would fall into the wrong hands—Asbeel's hands. But she had found me and changed everything. As soon as she had wrenched the stone from my possession, I wanted nothing more than to hold it again.

People filtered out of the low stone buildings that crammed both sides of the narrow lane. The bustle hardly slowed me, as I moved nimbly around the pressing crowd. Each building looked like the last, each beggar the same, as I dashed past them. The only constant in my vision was that fleeting speck of black, the flowing robe of the masked woman.

A man cut in front of me, but I darted between his legs, and he seemed not to notice my presence. I flew as if nothing could stop me, desperate not to lose my target in the swarm of brightly colored robes and exotic headwraps. If I lost track of the masked woman I would be adrift in the winding, confusing streets of Memnon. And somewhere out there, Asbeel hunted me.

I turned onto the next street, and there again was the flutter of the woman's cloak, just rounding a corner. There the road widened and brightened. A thin bit of smoke wafted into the street, and the noise and bustle increased tenfold. I hastened my step, knowing, fearing, what lay around that corner.

I reached the bend in a rush, and saw precisely what I had feared: an open market square, huge and packed with shoppers. Ahead, through the crowd, I saw her moving. The people hardly slowed her measured pace. I tried to push through the crowd, but it was no use.

She was escaping.

I could not follow.

I was lost.

I heard a flutter of wings behind me, and the crowd parted. Several voices cried out in a language I did not understand.

I turned, moving purely on instinct, my stiletto out, ready to face Asbeel again. As would surely be my lot in life, until one of us was dead.

But the wings did not belong to Asbeel.

Nine ravens, black as midnight, stared up at me. Eight had formed a circle on the ground, their wings stretched, touching tip to tip; but each had turned its head to me. The ninth stood in the middle, its chest puffed out proudly, and opened its beak.

But caw it did not. It spoke.

"Flee," said the bird. "Do not pursue."

I blinked a few times and looked around the street. No one around me seemed concerned by the strange events. They continued about their business, though they did give the birds a wide berth.

I stared at the bird, and it stared back at me. Feeling quite foolish, I asked the most obvious of questions. "Do not pursue whom?"

"Us." The bird's head twitched to one side.

"Why would I pursue you? Who are you?"

"Birds."

I could hardly find words. The situation seemed so ridiculous. "I'm not pursuing birds," I said. "I'm pursuing a thief."

"No thief," the bird said.

"A woman took something from me without permission. That makes her a thief." My eyes darted through the crowd's sea of colorful robes, desperate to catch a glimpse of the dark cloak.

The bird skittered toward me. "Savior. Do not pursue."

I stared directly into the raven's beady eyes. "How do you know about . . . any of this?" I asked.

"We see."

"You've been following me, haven't you?"

The raven nodded. The strange gesture sent a shiver up my arm.

"Then you're a spy, and no better than the thief." I advanced a step and brandished my sword menacingly.

The birds lifted off from the ground in a flurry of feathers, their wings beating at the air, throwing up a cloud of dust in their wake. Their caws—the cries of ordinary ravens, not words—faded rapidly into the distance.

With the birds gone, the crowd of shoppers pressed closer to me. I sheathed my sword and let myself fall into the flow.

I shook my head. Of all the bizarre creatures I had met on my journey, that had to be one of the strangest sights of all. A talking bird? At least it had not tried to hurt me. The bird—as odd as it was—seemed to want to help me, in its own strange way.

But I would not heed its warning. I would not give up on the stone. True, I had little to go on. I knew nothing of the thief who had stolen it. I had no magic to aid me. And I knew no one who did.

I let out a heavy sigh. Elbeth, Perrault. Everyone who had tried to help me was hurt, missing—or dead. I briefly considered returning to the docks. But the thought of facing *Sea Sprite*'s crew again filled my heart with shame.

Pirates hunting me had attacked the ship, and though we had won the battle, several crew had been killed, and the ship was damaged. Our victory came thanks only to Drizzt Do'Urden and his friends, who had disembarked the ship more than a day before. If I returned to *Sea Sprite* and brought on another attack, the crew would be overwhelmed. And I would never forgive myself.

The crowd pressed me on to the edge of the market. In my darkest days on board the ship, Drizzt had spoken to me about family—not the family you are born to, but the one you find. I knew he was talking about the crew of *Sea Sprite*, telling me that they were my family. I hung my head. Maybe I should return to the only family I had left and give up my foolish journey. The stone had caused me nothing but pain.

A feeling like a thousand tiny pinpricks shot up my arm. I shook my hand reflexively, and accidentally slapped the wide backside of a shopper passing beside me.

"Aii!" the woman shouted. "Keep your filthy hands to yourself!" She shoved my shoulder—hard.

I lost my balance and crashed into the side of a small tent at the edge of the market. The tent wall crumpled, and the pole it was attached to dropped directly on my head, dazing and blinding me. I stumbled forward and fell to the dusty ground.

A large hand, heavy and strong, grasped my shoulder. A deep, throaty laugh filled my ears.

Asbeel!

CHAPTER THREE

I thrashed about, only serving to further entrap myself. The tent cloth wrapped about my arm and entangled my legs. I felt like a fly in a spider's web, each movement only ensuring my demise. I tried in vain to grip the dagger in my belt to cut my way out of the trap. But I could not reach it.

A second hand joined the first, gripping me tightly, holding me still.

"Relax," said a deep voice, a voice not Asbeel's. "You try to move large, but you are trapped, so you move not at all. Move small, and you will move far."

"What in the world does that mean?" I asked, my voice muffled by the drapery.

"Be still," the voice said quietly—as quietly as a thunderstorm could be. "And I will help you."

The hands released me, tentatively. When I did not resume my struggle, they began slowly to unwrap the tangled mess I had become.

A few moments later I lay on the dusty floor inside the tent. Its remaining cotton walls rippled gently in the breeze. The fourth strip of fabric lay in a pile on the ground where I had tumbled into it. The air was hazy with smoke leaking from the pots of incense placed around the room.

"Greetings, maimed one," said an old man. He spoke with the cadence of a bear shambling through the forest: not in a rush to get anywhere, not wasting any energy where it wasn't needed; but with the confidence of a creature secure in its own great strength.

"How do you know my name?" I asked, climbing to my feet unsteadily.

"What?"

"My name. You called me Maimun." I took a step back. "How did you know my name?"

The man towered over me, his head nearly touching the top of the small tent. Everything about him seemed out of place in those tight quarters. "I called you 'maimed one.' Scarred one."

I felt him staring at my chest. My shirt had fallen open, revealing the long black patch across my chest. "Tar," I said. "To cauterize the wound."

"Yes, and it must have hurt greatly," said the man. "But I wasn't speaking of that wound. There is magic about you, and that is scarred as well, more than your flesh." He stepped closer, leaning heavily on a single bone, as tall as his shoulder, which in turn was as tall as most men. The great thing was blackened along one side, and from its top dangled feathers, claws, and teeth.

The hair on the back of my neck pricked up. "Who are you?" I asked.

"I have no name," he said.

I took another step back and glared at him. "How can you have no name?"

"I had a name once, but it was taken from me. I shall not get a new one until I rejoin my tribe in the next land." He raised his bone staff and pointed to a corner of the tent filled with pillows. "Now, come, Maimed One, sit with me a while, that I may look at you."

I glanced over my shoulder. Behind me, I could see the open street, filled with bustling shoppers, a clear path to escape should he attempt an attack. If I sat in the corner of his small tent, I would be in a much more dangerous position.

"You have questions, yes?" He said, smiling. "I can look at you and maybe see the answers." From behind his long hair, pale blue eyes, like the midwinter horizon a moment before dawn, stared at me, unblinking. I felt weak, naked, beneath his piercing gaze.

I shook my head. Had I truly fallen so far? Had Asbeel really chased me to such a frightened state? There was no doubt I needed help. I had no one else to turn to. Perhaps the man could tell me how to find the masked woman and retrieve the stone. I took a deep breath and decided to trust him.

As I sat down on the pile of pillows, a cloud of dust rose up, stinging my eyes and nose. The pillows were not as soft as they looked. I rubbed the new bruise on my thigh and shifted to a more comfortable position, as the old seer settled cross-legged on the bare floor in front of me.

I had witnessed divination magic in practice only once before: when Perrault's dwarf friend Alviss had used his crystal ball to allow me to spy on Perrault and his friend Jaide. I knew from various tomes that scrying often used such tools—a crystal ball, a mirror— to peer through to a distant place, so I scanned the room for any such object. But the space was sparse, almost bare. A chest sat against the wall opposite the tent's door (the proper entrance, not the fallen wall), with a stack of books atop it. I thought back to Perrault's collection of books, which I had taken such care to organize. The seer's books were stacked haphazardly; only three of the seven were spine-out, and those were in no particular order, with one of Volo's accounts sandwiched between what I could only assume was a spellbook and one written in a language I could not read.

Smoke wafted about the large man, drifting up from a lit candle set at his feet—where did it come from? Ever so slowly, the man began to rock back and forth; his lips moved, but I heard no sound. The smoky haze moved with him. His features wavered within it, and though I knew I could reach out and touch him, somehow I felt as if he was not fully there.

After a moment I found myself swaying in rhythm with him. A wave of calm washed over me.

I leaped to my feet, my eyes darting around the room. I felt as though I'd been startled awake from a long nap, though I was sure I hadn't been asleep. The old man's eyes flew open, and he took in a quick breath.

"What just happened?" I asked, trying to keep my voice steady.

"I looked at you, and someone looked back." He leaned heavily on his staff and rose up beside me.

"What do you mean, 'looked back'?" I asked.

He paused, as if searching for the words to explain. "I told you before, there is magic about you. I looked at you to find that magic and to follow it."

I nodded and gestured for him to speak more quickly. Suddenly, I felt as though there was no time to lose. "And what did you see? Did you find the magic?"

"No." The old man replied, not seeming to notice my panic. He spoke in the same measured pace. "Someone else was following the same line. He seeks what you seek."

"Who? What was his name?" I asked, then shook my head. Divination magic surely didn't work like that. The old man must be thinking me a fool. "I mean can you describe him?"

He nodded, and suddenly I felt less absurd. "A stranger to these lands, of skin and manner. Magical by nature, not by practice."

"That is all?" I said. "You see nothing more?"

The old seer picked up the candle and blew it out. "If you can find him, his journey will aid your own." He stared at the candlewick. "That is all I know."

I paced the tiny tent and flexed and unflexed my left hand, which tingled as if I'd sat on it too long. My mind was spinning, rolling over all the possibilities. Who could the magical person be?

The woman in the mask? I had no idea what her nature was, nor her skin, nor anything about her. But no, the seer had said "*he* seeks what you seek." The masked stranger already had what I sought. And she was female, that much I was sure of.

Did he mean Asbeel? The thought made my heart race. I scanned the crowds outside, but the demon was nowhere to be seen. Asbeel did seek the stone. But he also knew who had it. I thought back to when the woman in the mask had appeared in the alley. He had seemed to know her somehow, but I certainly couldn't ask Asbeel who she is. If I were to find him again, he would surely try to kill me. That thought sent cold chills up my spine.

I glanced again at the stack of books, at the Volo in particular. I recalled a passage in one of Volo's books describing one of the rarest sentient races seen on Toril's surface. "Creatures of magic themselves, they are in tune with the unique magical nature of the deepest parts of the world." The book described the various sub-races of the elves; the passage described the drow.

The drow. Magical by nature. Pitch black skin. Strangers to our world. I had only ever seen one drow in my life. He had entered the city only a day earlier to complete a journey of his own.

"Drizzt?" I raced toward the seer. "Was it Drizzt Do'Urden you saw?"

The seer gazed at me for what seemed like an eternity, and he slowly nodded. "It matters not what I see. It matters only what you feel."

With that I was certain. Drizzt was the answer. He was searching for the stone. And to find it, all I had to do was find him.

CHAPTER FOUR

I pushed my way to the edge of the market crowd, and found myself staring down a lane to the city gate—or rather a hole in the wall that served as a gate—to a road out into a sandy wasteland. Four guards flanked the portal, leaning lazily against the cool stone of the wall, staying in the shade.

I ran to the gate, passing a group of beggars along the side of the road. As I passed, they pleaded for scraps and coins, but I did not slow my pace. "Hey," I called. "Hey, guard!"

If Drizzt and his friends had left the city here, the guards would know it; if not, I would attempt to navigate the maze of the city to another gate, and so on.

None of the guards stirred as I approached. I wondered for a moment if they were asleep.

I cleared my throat. "Excuse me? Guard!"

At last the biggest man spoke. He scarcely moved a muscle, as if he had perfected the art of pure laziness. "Go away, beggar rat," he said.

I stepped closer. "I am no beggar. And I need some help."

He opened one eye. "You look like a beggar, and it ain't my job to help."

"It's your job to protect the people of the city. And I don't look like a beggar. Have you ever seen a beggar with a cloak like this?" I waved Perrault's magical royal-blue cloak, exposing the finely-crafted hilt of Perrault's dagger, belted at my hip.

The guard stood and faced me. "You're right, I suppose. You don't look like a beggar. You look like a thief." He took a step forward, trying to appear menacing. He stopped to rub the sleep from his eyes, and I nearly laughed aloud, but thought better of it.

The guard would be of no use to me, I knew. And I needed some answers—now.

"Any of you, then," I said, turning back to the row of beggars on the street. "Any of you see a dr—" I nearly said drow, but caught myself, remembering that Drizzt would surely be wearing his magical mask. "Any of you see an elf come through here, probably with a dwarf and two humans?"

After a moment, no one answered, so I moved farther down the lane and repeated my question.

Someone answered, a boy who looked to be about half my age. I winced when he stepped forward. Dirt coated his face and bare chest. His ribs showed through his hollow chest. "Yeah, I seen 'em." His voice was weak, almost flimsy. "Elf, woman, dwarf, giant."

My heart leaped. "That's them!" I fished around in my pocket for coins, and found three, all silver. I brought one out and presented it to the boy. All the other beggars perked up at the sight and began moving toward me. I ignored them. "A silver for you if you can tell me where they went and how to find them."

"They left the city through them gates," he said. "I dunno where they's heading." He smiled, for no reason I could see.

"Where does that gate lead then?" I asked.

"I dunno. The Calim Desert, I suppose. Get a camel and follow 'em." He held out his hand.

I placed the coin in it, but did not let go. "Who sells camels?" I asked.

"Lotsa folks sell camels."

"Who near here?"

The boy thought for a second, then pointed down a side street. "Sali Dalib, he sells camels. His tent is at the next market down that road," he said. I released the coin, and the boy scampered off into the shadows.

Sali Dalib's tent stood almost directly in front of the street, just as it opened into a relatively small market square. The large pavilion had recently been damaged, I saw, as two men worked on a makeshift scaffold raising one side of it. Outside there was an empty enclosure, for camels I assumed.

A goblin sat beside the door. He held a small bag to his head. His face was discolored around the bag—a bruise, I realized. In his other hand was a small wand. He pointed it at me, briefly and subtly. I pretended not to notice as I approached.

"We are not open, no, no," said a voice from within. A man in a brightly-colored flowing robe and a shining yellow turban came outside. He carried a large traveler's pack as if he were heading out on a long journey. "No food for de beggars today, no, no. Go away." He shooed me away, but the goblin grabbed his robe and whispered. The man stopped.

"But perhaps we can make an exception. Yes, yes, we can," he said. "You wish to buy, yes, yes? Or maybe to trade?" His voice rose an octave as he spoke, his tone switching from the gruff dismissal of a beggar to a honeyed sales pitch now that he considered me a potential customer. Perrault had always told me to judge a person by their actions when they have nothing to gain from you; by that standard, I did not much like Sali Dalib.

I opened my mouth to speak, but the man cut me off. "Inside. We should talk inside, yes, yes," he said, closing the few feet to me in the blink of an eye and putting his arm around my shoulders. He herded me to the tent. The goblin followed behind, quietly.

"I be Sali Dalib, purveyor of de finest wares, yes, yes! I have everything you need, at de bestest prices in de whole city!"

The interior of the tent looked much like the exterior: fine silk in many mismatched colors pieced together somewhat haphazardly. It would have been a fine shop, were it not partially destroyed. On one side of the tent lay a mess of broken trinkets, shelves, and ropes. On the other side a case of magical instruments caught my eye.

Sali Dalib hopped over to the shelf, following my gaze. "You wish to buy a Doss lute? I have one on sale cheap!"

I opened my mouth to answer, but Sali Dalib had already moved to the next shelf. "Or perhaps a nice traveling cloak? You already have one, yes, yes, but dis one is so much finer!" He held up a coarse yellow cloak, patched in several places. "We can trade, yes, yes!"

"How about some broken shelves?" I asked sarcastically, looking past him at the shelves and ropes scattered around the floor. "You seem to have a lot of those."

"Yes, yes, we have many," he said, apparently not catching the joke. "A minor accident, we had, yes, yes. How many would you like?" He beamed at me, bouncing up and down slightly in obvious anticipation, until his turban slipped and fell over his eyes.

R.A. & GENO SALVATORE

"None. I just want information," I said. I could almost feel Sali Dalib's expression drop.

He pulled his turban up, eyes narrowed. "Information about what?" he asked. His voice, so round and robust before, was utterly flat.

"About an elf. He would have been traveling with two humans—a small woman and a huge man—and a dwarf." I meant to continue, but a groan from behind me—from the goblin—cut me off.

Sali Dalib stared at me. "You be friend of de drow?" he snarled.

"Friend? Not really, I'm just looking for—" I choked on my own words. He had identified Drizzt as a drow. "So you did meet them?" I asked, trying not to show the trepidation I was feeling.

"Friend of de drow is not welcome here," Sali Dalib said, standing up as straight and as tall as he could manage and pointing at the door.

"Wait, wait, I'm not his friend," I said. "I'm looking for him. He owes me gold." It was an outright lie, of course, but I figured perhaps I could connect with Sali Dalib in terms he could relate to. "I just need to know where he went."

"Calimport," the goblin gurgled behind me.

I rolled my eyes—of course they were headed to Calimport. "I mean, how? By what path?"

"By camel, yes, yes. By de caravan—" Sali Dalib's voice seemed to lighten mid sentence. "No, no, not de caravan road, by de bestest road." The goblin groaned again, but Sali Dalib shot him a glare, and he stifled his complaint.

"The bestest road?" I parroted.

"Yes, yes, de bestest road. It be marked by signs. Yes, yes, just outside the city, and it be de fastest and safest road to Calimport! De bestest, it be! That be why they call it de bestest road, yes, yes!" Sali Dalib was positively beaming at that point. "You need a camel, yes, yes. Sali Dalib will sell you a camel and cheap, yes, yes."

"I have no money." I would have felt worse about the lie if I were not so sure Sali Dalib was trying to swindle me.

Sali Dalib did not miss a beat. "A trade then, yes, yes? A camel for . . . " he looked at the goblin. "For your cape? It be a cape from de North, yes, yes, to keep you warm. But in de south it be warm anyway!"

"In the south, a good cloak keeps the sun off so you don't die of heat," I replied. "I'd not make it far in the desert without a cloak."

"We throw in a Calishite cloak then, yes, yes, And de deal is done!" Sali Dalib clapped his hands loudly, excitedly, and bounced over to the shelf with the ugly old cloak. He turned back to me, holding the ragged thing aloft, to see me shaking my head.

"I can't trade this cloak," I said. "It belonged to my father, and I can't part with it."

Again, and instantly, Sali Dalib's eyes narrowed, and his voice flattened. It amazed me how quickly he seemed to swing between incredible excitement and a seething anger. "Den we are at an impasse," he said.

"Maybe you can loan me a camel?" I said. "I told you, the drow owes me gold. I'll pay you for your help once I collect."

Sali Dalib started to answer, then stopped, then started again, then stopped again, until finally his goblin cohort answered for him. "Camel can die. Not a good loan."

"How is it going to die?" I asked. "Are you trying to sell me a sick camel?" I tried to sound angry.

"Maybe drow kills it."

Sali Dalib was nodding again. "Yes, yes, camel can die and drow maybe kills it or steals it. Yes, yes. But maybe we loan something else?" He bustled over to the shelf with the lute, but ducked behind it. I heard the click of a trunk lid opening, then some shuffling as the merchant rummaged through a container.

"Here, dese bestest boots in de city! Make you run faster! You run on de bestest road, catch drow, and make him pay, yes, yes. Give Sali Dalib his fair cut, yes, yes!" He held up a pair of boots, a skin of water, and an open sack holding enough dried bread to last a few days. It was not much, I saw, perhaps enough for a day or two. It would certainly not get me anywhere near Calimport, no matter how fast the boots would make me run.

But I nodded and accepted the objects as he presented them. "I'll bring them back soon," I said.

"You will, yes, yes! With money to pay me for a camel, too! You look trusty, yes, yes!" he said

"Trustworthy," the goblin muttered quietly, doubtfully.

I was suspicious. But I had no other choice, surely no better choice, so I accepted his boots and his far-too-vigorous handshake, and I bid Sali Dalib farewell.

I returned to the same gate where the guards had brushed me off but an hour earlier, and found them standing in exactly the same positions as when I had left. None of them batted an eye as I strode forward to the gate. None of them said a word as I left the city. But I could feel their eyes on me, and I knew what they were thinking, because the thought crossed my mind as well.

A single traveler, without a mount, with few rations, heading into the desert alone. I had no chance.

But I also had no choice. Drizzt had only a slight head start, but I would have to hurry if I wanted to catch him. I could waste no more time gathering supplies.

I said a quick prayer to Tymora—though I doubted that any of the gods would watch over me, she seemed the best bet—and walked out onto the hot sands of the Calim Desert.

CHAPTER FIVE

I had read of deserts, had occasionally been in cities on the edge of them, had endured the heat of crowded Memnon for the past two days. But the truth of the desert—the scorching heat, the shifting sands, and the utter dryness of the land—had never reached me through my books.

I traveled all afternoon, stopping only to take a sip of water or a small bite of stale bread every so often. But I hadn't covered much ground. Each time I came to the crest of a dune and turned around, I could still see Memnon there in the distance. Yet my feet and legs ached as if I had marched a hundred miles. The sands of the desert provided no solid surface to step on. Each stride felt like walking across a soft mattress. My boots sank into the sand, and I pulled them back out, again and again and again.

Not far outside Memnon's gate, I passed a sign, written sloppily, reading "De Bestest Road" with an arrow pointing east, not south.

Instantly I knew Sali Dalib had no intention that I would ever reach Calimport. I had read about such deceptions in my books. Had I followed his directions and taken "De Bestest Road," I would have been intercepted by some of his minions. All Sali Dalib had to do was alert them to the presence of the boots, and his "loan" would be recovered, along with everything of mine he coveted: Perrault's cloak, my dagger—and quite possibly my life. And so I passed the sign and kept walking south.

The sun, thankfully, proved less of an obstacle than I had feared. Despite Sali Dalib's warnings, my cloak proved ample protection from the brutal rays. I kept the hood up and the cowl low to keep the glare out of my eyes. I had always known Perrault's cloak carried some protective magic—he had used it to sever the mental connection Asbeel had placed upon me during a fight on Baldur's Gate's docks—but on that trudge through the desert I came to believe its protective magic extended much further. But even with the cloak beating back the worst of the sun, I was sweating profusely and going through my water far more rapidly than I wished.

Dehydration, not heat, was the greatest danger of the desert. I had walked only a few miles, only half a day, with at least seven more days to go, and had spent nearly half my water.

And the boots Sali Dalib had loaned me were obviously fakes. Then again, I was a fake in the manner I had borrowed—or, rather, had stolen—them. I had no intention of ever giving them back.

But I was justified, I told myself. Sali Dalib had meant to have me killed, to take back what he had lent me and more. He had lied to me, and I had lied to him; he had tried to steal from me, and I had stolen from him.

I wondered what Perrault would think of me now.

Would he approve of my theft? Probably, I thought. I recognized Sali Dalib for what he was and cheated the cheater. But Perrault probably would have lamented that such a decision had been necessary. He wished to protect me, in everything he did—not just from demons, but from the necessity of compromising my principles.

I remembered the lesson he had tried to teach me after we fled Asbeel in Baldur's Gate. Perrault had lied to the captain of a ship to get us onboard and had attempted to change the captain's course in order to facilitate his goals.

His goals. My safety. "You protect first those you love, then yourself, then everyone else," he had said.

Perrault's lie to the captain had disgusted me then; yet perhaps I finally understood his lesson. I myself had lied, and I had been rewarded.

That memory led to another: Joen, her hair flowing in the sea breeze from her perch high atop the mainmast, in the crow's nest of the ship; of her smiling as she tossed a hunk of bread up to the circling gulls, that they might share her mirth; of her eyes, staring in silence at the sunset.

Of her wrists, bound in chains, as she was led belowdecks on the pirate ship.

On the ship Perrault had called.

To protect me.

Abruptly I stopped and shook my head, as if I could shake loose the painful memories. The sun had gone down, and the night air was much cooler, cold even. My legs ached, but I decided to press on.

Travel in the desert at night was much cooler than during the day, but no less difficult. The sand still shifted beneath my feet, and the desert creatures, which stayed hidden beneath it through the hot hours under the baking sun, came out in force as night fell.

I drew my stiletto and enacted its magic, lighting the blade with a blue flame. I was pleased to see the fire worked even when the weapon was not in its sword form. My blazing blade provided sufficient light to move by, and occasionally revealed a strange beast: a whip-tailed scorpion; a small, quick lizard with teeth too large for its mouth; a snake that skittered sideways. Each time I saw an animal, it moved quickly away from my light. But I was reminded that there could be another right behind me, following in my shadow.

I tried to keep such thoughts from my mind—and thoughts of the rarer, larger monsters of the desert, which I had read of in my books—but as my weariness grew I found I could not push the dark beasts from my mind.

And even darker thoughts crept in. Why was Drizzt searching for the stone? How could I really be certain that he would help me if I found him? What if he wanted the stone for himself and killed me to keep me from stopping him?

Drizzt had been in my presence along with the stone for some time on *Sea Sprite*. In fact, he had sat beside me when I was lying helpless in bed, seriously wounded. If he had wanted the stone, he could have taken it then. Had I hidden it that well? Perhaps he had known I had it all along and concealed his intentions, fooling me into trusting him until the time was right to steal the stone—or to trick me into giving it to him. I gulped. Was Drizzt in league with Asbeel? I glanced up at the sky, half expecting to see the demon here, following me. . . .

I broke into a light jog. I tried my best to maintain a southerly heading, using the stars to guide me. Perrault had taught me how to navigate by the night sky, but I had never tried it on my own. All through the night I worried I had lost my way. By the time my strength failed me and the horizon grew light, I had no way of knowing whether I was on course or far, far off.

When the sun rose, directly to my left, I breathed a sigh of relief. I had stayed true, and had made good ground to the south. Safe in that knowledge, and too tired to do anything about it anyway, I took a few sips of water and a bite of bread and lay down, wrapping Perrault's magical cloak around me to stave off the sun as I slept.

And so I continued toward Calimport and the only hope I had left. By night, I trudged through the shifting sand, dark thoughts crowding my mind. By day, I slept under the protection of Perrault's cloak.

On the third night, my waterskin ran dry. Sometime that same night, I dropped the sack with my old boots and my food ration in it. The weight only slowed me down, and dry food was no good without water.

But I walked on.

I felt the sweat bead on my neck as the sun rose on the fourth day. I did not stop to sleep. I was not halfway to Calimport, but was too far from Memnon to turn around. And I knew if I lay down, I would never rise again. The hot wind whipped the sand into a frenzy, obscuring my vision. It diffused the light but amplified the heat of the blazing orb above me.

But I walked on.

The wind stopped suddenly. The sand fell to rest, and the dry air sucked the moisture from my breath before it left my lungs. I pulled the cowl of my cloak over my head, and I could not see the sun, but I could feel it still, reflecting off the hot sands to bypass my magical cloak's protection. My legs burned, my knees felt weak. I stopped sweating. My body had run out of water.

But I walked on. And I was not alone.

Perrault walked beside me, humming a tune, matching my pace. I tried to remember the words that went with the melody, but they were in Elvish, and I could not recall them.

Jaide, the most beautiful woman I had seen in my life, walked beside me, her hand resting gently on my shoulder. She tried to assure me that I would be all right. But her words did little to comfort me.

Ahead of me, Drizzt Do'Urden strode with purpose—white hair, jet black skin, and two swords belted at his hip. Drizzt had lied to me, had hidden his intentions from me. I sought him to confront him. Strength flowed out from him, yet it was not enough to keep my spirit alive.

No, it was the most unexpected companion who saved me. Her hair flowed in a wind that did not exist, long strands of wheat whipping about, without a care, free. A bird sat on her arm, picking at a loaf of bread in her other hand. After what seemed like days, Joen turned to me and beckoned, motioning to her eyes, then to the horizon.

I followed her gaze, over the dunes to the east, away from the descending sun. Through the hot haze it took me a while to see what she had seen, but there it was, clear as could be.

Trees.

Trees meant water.

Water meant life.

I looked back to Joen, but she was not there. Nor was Drizzt. I turned to Perrault, but he was gone, and Jaide's hand no longer rested on my shoulder. The sun beat down on me.

But the trees remained.

CHAPTER SIX

As I moved closer to the trees, my vision cleared, and my heart beat faster. I was not dreaming them, could not be dreaming them. The oasis was real—a small spring of water, barely a pond, surrounded by a few tall trees. They were not like the trees to the north, but were thinner and without branches until the top, where several great fronds extended into a natural umbrella. My heart lifted at the sight. The oasis had water, and shelter, and possibly food if those trees bore any fruit.

Along the northern side of the pond, I saw a group of men had set camp right at the shore. I suddenly felt nauseous. There were at least two dozen men, all wearing brightly colored clothing, their heads wrapped in cloth, presumably to beat back the sun. A dozen unsaddled horses milled about, chewing the thin mossy grass growing by the pond's shore, or sipping at the water.

Each man carried a sword or spear. Each had rough, gnarled facial hair and was covered in dust, as if he had not seen a town in months. There were no women with them, unless they were hiding in the tents.

Bandits. There was a good chance they held the water hole, and would share only if I paid the toll. I considered my own meager funds. I had two silver coins left—certainly not enough. I wished I could wait until nightfall, when it would be so much easier to sneak past, but my thirst would not wait. I had to go immediately, or I would never make it.

I stayed low to the ground as I crested the last dune before the oasis, feeling fully exposed. The pond was no more than ten yards across in any direction, more a glorified puddle than a true lake. The sight of the water made my throat ache. But how would I reach its shore without being spotted? I crawled down the dune with the sun directly at my back.

The trees had thin trunks, but on the south-western corner of the pond they formed a dense grove. I slipped in between the trees, moving as quickly as I dared.

I placed my hand upon one of the tall trees, feeling the roughness of its bark, delighting in the sensation, in any sensation besides sand. Suddenly, commotion broke out from the bandit camp.

I scrambled behind the tree. I heard mugs clanging loudly. I glanced around the trunk and breathed a sigh of relief. The bandits were toasting. Water sloshed over the sides of their cups. What could have so excited bandits such as those, I tried not to imagine. I hoped they were merely happy about the discovery of a water source, not about the death and robbery of their victims. But that was not my immediate concern. My immediate concern was the utter dryness of my throat, the pounding behind my temples, the weakness of my legs, the aching in my joints. I needed water, and I needed it right away. So whatever they were toasting, I was glad for their distraction.

I dropped flat to my belly. The sand was covered by a springy sort of short grass. I pulled myself along, arm over arm, making hardly a whisper and staying as low to the ground as possible. I inched along until finally I pulled myself right to the edge of the water.

I drank deeply, gulping down water like I had never seen it before, like I had been parched my whole life. I dipped my hands in the water, and then my face. I let out a sigh, then stifled it until I realized the loud celebration continued, and no one could possibly have heard me. I silently toasted the bandits, feeling like I deserved to join their celebration. Then I filled my belly until it sloshed.

"Hey," said a voice behind me. "That water ain't yours."

I froze. "It's water. It's everyone's," I replied quietly. I subtly drew my dagger as I turned, tucking it tight against my wrist and keeping my hand beneath my cloak.

"Not in the desert it ain't," said the man. He was dressed like the others at the camp, in a bright red tunic and simple, functional breeches and boots. His head was wrapped in a slightly darker red turban, which had come partially unwound, but he seemed hardly to notice. His face would have been rough even without the days of stubble growing on it.

"I'm sorry, I didn't realize," I said. "I'll just move along, then."

"No, you won't," he said, his voice emotionless. "Not 'til you pay me what I'm owed."

"Are you the toll-man, then? The leader of these ban—?" I interrupted myself, before I could say "bandits," hoping he would not catch my slip.

He scoffed. " 'Course not. I'm the lookout. But right now I'm the guy you're gonna pay not to kill you." His eyes were dark and menacing and, I thought, merciless.

"Looks like they're having a party over there." I said, motioning to the ongoing celebration. "Why weren't you invited?"

"I see what you're trying to do, kid, and you might as well stop now. It don't work like you think it works, got it? I like being the lookout. It lets me collect from the wretches like you who stumble over here while the others are busy, and don't no one else take a cut."

I considered pushing further, trying to drive a wedge between him and his cohorts, or perhaps threatening to reveal his scam to the rest of his crew. But something in the man's eyes made me stop. He knew I was powerless. There was nothing I could say that would turn him away.

I leaped to my feet, then immediately doubled over in pain. My belly ached, my head ached, my very skin ached. I wondered what dark magic the man was using on me. Then I realized. The water I had just consumed was working its way into my system, trying to rehydrate me far too fast.

The bandit laughed and held forward his long spear, its barbed tip glinting in the last rays of daylight. "Now, you gonna pay me, or am I gonna take the coin from your corpse?"

I swallowed the bile bubbling up in my throat. "If you want my silver," I said, "you'll have to come claim it." I snapped my hand forward, lengthening the stiletto into a fine saber.

"Well all right then, kid, if you insist." The bandit came at me, his spear tip leading.

I whipped my sword up and out, pushing aside the thrusting spear, and moved to lunge forward. But with a simple twist of his wrists the man reset the spear, its tip directly in my path. I stopped and pulled back, shuffling a step to the left to stay ahead of the prodding spear.

The bandit circled with me, his feet crossing over in perfect harmony. He jabbed again. I blocked easily, tapping my sword against the shaft of the spear and redirecting its head aside. Still I held no illusions about my fighting prowess. I knew the bandit was testing me.

Steel crashed against wood. With each motion, a wave of nausea washed over me, and with each impact, the fingers of my left hand tingled. After each thrust and parry, I took a step to my left, and the bandit did the same, and soon we had reversed positions, with his back to the water and mine to the desert.

I hoped that the sound of our battle would not carry above the loud celebration. I could still hear the loud laughter and mugs clanging. I considered running. But I doubted I could outrun the man in my current state, let alone the horses he could send after me. No, I needed to win the fight, and I needed to do so quietly, without alerting the other bandits.

But the task was not a simple one. The bandit had apparently taken enough of my measure. He jabbed again, but even before I had finished my parry he retracted his spear, moved his trailing right hand over his left, and stepped forward. I found my sword out of position as he stepped and lunged, his spear tip covering the three feet to me in the blink of an eye.

I fell back, and threw up my hand in desperation. And somehow, I clipped the shaft of the spear to raise it harmlessly over my head.

I stumbled backward. The bandit brought his hands up and thrust the spear brutally toward me.

I fell flat on my back to avoid the wicked tip. Its barbs glinted in the setting sun. Suddenly I knew what to do.

I somersaulted backward. The bandit came at me again. I came to my feet just as he lunged forward for the third time, and I brought my sword to bear.

I did not try to parry. Instead, I brought my sword up under the thrusting spear and hooked my blade right at the hilt against the spear's barbs. In the same motion, I dropped my trailing shoulder. I rolled my sword over myself, pulling with all my strength and weight.

The man was perfectly balanced to thrust his spear. But his feet were not set to resist my tug. I rolled all the way around, pulling him forward, pulling us together, pulling his spear past my body. When our momentum played itself out, we found ourselves barely four inches apart. I was far inside his spear's reach, but my sword was out wide.

I expected him to try to retreat, to reset his spear, and to continue the fight. So I moved forward. I brought my sword in tight, hoping to get at least one good strike, to win the fight right there. But he did not retreat. He dropped his spear and stepped forward, wrapping his arms tight around me.

I struggled a moment, but could not even begin to break his clinch. He was strong. Not abnormally strong, not as strong as Asbeel or the strange pirate who had pulled me off *Sea Sprite* into Memnon's harbor. But the bandit was a man, and I a boy, and he had the better position: his arms were wrapped all the way around me, pressing my own arms tight against my body.

I felt as though he would crush the life out of me. Each time I exhaled, he squeezed tighter. Each breath was more difficult than the last.

I had only one option left. I held up my sword and put it flat on his back. He barely seemed to notice. I had neither the angle nor the strength to try to stab him with it.

But I did not need to stab him. I thought of blue fire, and suddenly my sword was ablaze.

The bandit screamed. I fell to the ground, gulping down air.

I looked at my fallen foe and gripped my sword, preparing to continue the fight. But he lay curled in a ball, weeping.

I jumped to my feet and spat, the taste of sour bile still lingering in my mouth,. "I guess you won't be taking coins from my corpse then, will you?" I said. And that's when I saw the bandit's back, where the fire had burned him. His tunic had been torn open, and his skin was bright red and blistering, as if badly sunburned. The torn clothes were wet. The bandit rolled over, and he howled again.

The camp across the pond was silent. But only for a second.

Then all sorts of commotion broke out. I glanced across the oasis to see the rest of the bandits running to their horses, saddles and bridles in hand. Others ran at me along both banks of the pond.

The nausea came back up again, and I did not fight it. I vomited, and though the bile burned at my throat, it felt somehow good.

Then I turned and ran full speed into the desert.

CHAPTER SEVEN

The sounds of the oasis receded behind me as fast as the top edge of the sun disappeared beneath the western horizon. My strides were long—impossibly long—like a deer bounding through the forest. My boots did not sink into the loose sand; they barely left a footprint even. "They make you run faster," Sali Dalib had said. I had thought them a hoax. But I had never even tried running.

I sprinted until my lungs burned before stopping to catch my breath. I stared down at my waterskin, hanging from my belt, empty.

I had been right at the watering hole and had not filled the skin, and I felt truly the fool for it. Calimport was no less than five days away from me, and I would not survive that long without water. I would have to wait a day and try to sneak back, hoping the bandits had moved on.

But as it turned out, I would not have the chance. I caught the faint sound of approaching hoofbeats, muffled by the sand. I turned to look only seconds before six men on horses, three brandishing spears and three carrying torches, crested the sand dune not thirty yards behind me.

I forced my tired legs to move, one then the other, as fast as they could carry me. I skipped across the surface of the sand, while my pursuers dug in with every galloping stride, throwing up a great cloud of dust behind them.

But horses were still faster than I. After mere moments they were around me, beside me.

A rider prodded at me with a spear. "Thief! Stop!"

He narrowly missed my arm. I could hardly breathe, and I feared I might vomit again. I glanced ahead through the shifting sands, but I saw nowhere I could hide. Panic rose in my chest.

I remembered seeing a fox chase a rabbit once, when I lived with Elbeth in the forest. The fox was faster than the rabbit, and whenever the chase moved in a straight line, the fox would gain ground. But the rabbit was more agile, and changed direction often, never allowing the fox a good straight line to run.

I would have to be as the rabbit.

I planted both my feet and leaped out to my side as forcefully as I could. My magical boots pushed hard against the loose sand, propelling me out and away. I hardly lost momentum despite my sharp turn.

The horses could not shift so quickly. They skidded and stomped right past the spot where I had pivoted.

I changed direction again, turning sharply to my right. The horses tried in vain to keep up with my darting movements. Just like the rabbit and the fox.

Of course, I couldn't help but think of the end result of that chase. The fox had caught the rabbit, and I had been given a lesson on the laws of the natural world: win, or die.

I turned to my left, and four of the six horses changed to follow. The other two, one with a spear and one with a torch, continued in a straight line. Soon they were far out to my side.

I cut hard right, and two of the four turned with

me, and suddenly I knew my folly. The horses running in straight lines stayed even with me, flanked me.

"Nowhere to go now, thief. No way to get past us," a bandit said. He wasn't wrong, but his high-pitched squeaky voice made him seem less frightening.

Two behind, two right, two left. I could not turn, or I would run into the flankers; I could not reverse, or I would meet the pursuit. And I could not outrun the horses if I stayed to my course.

My path led straight up the side of a great, tall dune, and I saw the flanking pairs moving farther out from me, to stay low around the mound. Horses would not travel so well up the dune. I could use the terrain to my advantage.

My legs ached, but I pushed them on, running as fast as I could in a straight line, directly for the top of the dune. The flankers were at least a hundred yards to my sides, whooping and hollering and staying dead even with me. The riders behind me stayed close, but on the uphill I gained some distance. On the downhill, I knew, I would be caught.

So I would not reach the downhill. As soon as I crested the top of the dune, I dug both my feet into the sand and drove myself to a halt. I felt my left leg go numb, felt my knee shift, but I ignored the pain. I turned fully around, facing directly at the oncoming riders.

And I leaped.

I leaped as no human is meant to leap. High and far and fast I soared through the desert air. I cleared the riders and horses by several yards, and landed so lightly I could hardly believe it, so lightly I did not even break stride. I heard the riders yelling and the horses whinnying. I heard a thud. I glanced over my shoulder and saw a torch, and the man holding it, lying on the ground, and one of the horses milling about.

I smiled. I am the rabbit, I thought again. But I beat the fox.

I crested the next rise to a beautiful view of the moon rising over the desert, appearing huge and bright and beautiful. I slowed my pace to a jog and listened carefully for hoofbeats, but I heard none.

My throat burned, and my tongue felt thick. My thirst nearly overwhelmed me. I had no choice but to stop and catch my breath. Perhaps they would not try to follow me, I thought. Perhaps I was in the clear. But the thought did nothing to comfort me. Bandits or no bandits, I would never make it to Calimport without water. To make matters worse, the wind picked up, howling and cold.

I wrapped my cloak tight around my shoulders. If I died here in the desert, at least I could say I had fought with honor at the oasis. I smiled at the memory of my final maneuver. The bandit had not even noticed me drawing my blade, let alone the blue fire, burning his back and leaving his tunic torn and wet.

I drew my blade, still its in saber form, and stared at it for a long moment. I took in a short breath. Could it be? I wondered. I ripped my cloak from my back and whipped it around the blade. With a thought, I lit the sword. The blue fire did not burn through the cloak. But when I unwrapped the blade, I saw something spectacular.

A layer of frost had formed on the blue fabric and it was quickly melting. Melting into precious water. I folded the cloak to make a trough, put my mouth against one end, and tilted it. Water trickled down, sweet and pure.

Again and again I lit my blade and nearly danced as the frost melted to a puddle on my cloak. But as thirsty as I was, I forced myself to drink slowly, letting the water settle in my stomach before sipping again. Once I had drunk my fill, I wrapped the cloak around my body and set off again at a jog, headed south.

CHAPTER EIGHT

Over the past several tendays my idea of a city had continually expanded. Despite my young life spent traveling with Perrault, I had never been in a city until a month before, when we had entered Baldur's Gate. Until then I had never seen so many people living so close together. Then I had sailed into Memnon harbor and seen a true sprawl. Miles of city, of buildings and makeshift shacks, rich and poor, were thrown together in a huge crowd. Baldur's Gate could have fit inside Memnon several times over. But even Memnon had not prepared me for my first view of Calimport.

Beneath the rising sun, the largest city on the face of Toril spread out before me, as endless as the sea beyond it. A million people must live there, I thought.

I walked down the last dune before the city gates. The wrought-iron bars were capped with golden spikes, each likely worth more than the average citizen's lifetime earnings.

I was weary and starving. I hadn't eaten in six days, since the night before the oasis. But I felt so elated by the end of my long road through the desert, I practically jogged into town. The guards, like those in Memnon nearly a tenday earlier, barely spared a glance.

The children, on the other hand, stared.

They reminded me of the boy in Memnon who had pointed me to Sali Dalib. They were thin, waifish, wearing whatever clothes they had stolen or salvaged, if any at all. Their skin was burnt, their bellies swollen with hunger. They stared at me as I walked past, not expectantly but hopefully.

I fished about in my pocket for my last two silver coins and moved to one of the several carts of food and supplies that lined the street. The fat vendor grinned as I handed him the coins, and without a word I took the two largest loaves of bread from his cart and moved away. I had certainly overpaid, but I was in no mood to haggle. I needed food, and I needed information, and the bread would get me both, I hoped.

The children, predictably, followed me, their hands out. A round-faced boy hung back in the shadows, watching. He looked about eight years old, larger than the others and healthier. Their leader, I guessed.

"Listen up," I said after I had led them all down a lonely road off the main entrance to the city, far from the guards' prying eyes. "You can all have some food if you help me. I'm looking for an elf by the name of Drizzt Do'Urden. He'll be with two humans, a man and a woman, and a dwarf with a red beard. Do you know where I might find him?"

A hush fell over the kids. I had expected to get a flood of responses, and to have to sift through a dozen false leads to hopefully find the one truthful one. But they were obviously frightened. I broke a piece of bread off, and they all stared at it, practically drooling. They were also obviously hungry.

One boy stepped up to me. I gripped my dagger, half worried that he might try to challenge me for the bread.

"No food's worth that fight," he said. He motioned to the rest of the children, and they all turned and shambled back to the gate, leaving me alone on the side of the road holding my bread.

I sat down on the dusty cobblestones, feeling much like a beggar myself. Had I been thinking clearly, I would have found some more people to question and continued my search for Drizzt. But I was holding two loaves of fresh bread. My stomach grumbled. By the time I fully realized I had taken a bite, I was brushing the last crumbs of the second loaf from my lap.

I breathed a satisfied sigh and looked up to find a boy right in front of me. It was the child who had hung back, watching from the shadows.

"You're looking for the drow," he whispered.

I started to nod, then stopped. "Elf. I never said drow."

"You don't have to say it. And you shouldn't be asking about him." He leaned his hand on the wall above me, and tilted his head toward the end of the road. He looked like all the other urchins on the street: dark hair, tanned skin bearing witness to years without shelter, oversized clothes probably stolen from a drunk passed out in an alley. But there was something different, something odd, about his eyes. "Entreri claimed him."

"What's an Entreri?"

He nearly choked and staggered back a step as if he'd been slapped in the face. He started to speak and stopped several times before finally managing a sentence. "You can't be walking around Calimport and not know the rules," he said.

"What rules?" I asked, scrambling to stand beside him. I wasn't exactly tall for my age, but still I towered nearly a foot above him.

"The rules of the streets, kid. The rules the pashas make. And the first rule is, don't cross Entreri."

"So Entreri is a person, then?"

"Yeah." The boy kicked a loose stone down the narrow road before turning back to look up at me. "Used to be, at least."

"Used to be? Is he undead?"

"I meant it figuratively. But he's as cold as the undead, that's for sure." The boy let out a short laugh. I couldn't help but stare as deep wrinkles creased the corners of his eyes.

"Who are you?" we both asked at the same time.

I waited a second, but he didn't answer. "My name is Maimun," I said.

"Twice lucky." He stared at me, studying my face. "That's a desert name, but you don't look like a desert person."

I nodded. "I suppose I am now, since I crossed the Calim on foot alone."

"You crossed the desert alone, looking for the drow? Gutsy, kid, but not too smart."

"Why do you keep calling me 'kid'? I'm probably older than you."

He chuckled. "Not a chance, kid." Again his skin crinkled around his eyes, and that time I was sure he wanted me to see it.

I took a step toward him and jabbed my finger at his chest. "You're not a kid," I said. "You're a halfling."

"And you're perceptive," he said, pushing my hand aside. "Been a street kid for about twenty years. Name's Dondon."

"You pretend to be a kid so you can rob travelers. So why tell me your secret?"

"So you'll believe me when I tell you to drop your search. Besides, you don't have anything worth stealing. I already checked."

I instinctively patted myself down—cloak, weapon, all there. Somehow I felt offended that he didn't consider those things worth stealing.

"Too hard to fence," the halfling said with a wink. He started walking down the road.

"Wait!" I ran after him. "Why do you care? Why are you telling me this?"

He chuckled again, but kept walking. "I don't care if you get yourself killed, kid."

I put my hands on my hips. "I can handle myself, you know."

Dondon kept walking until he reached the street corner. Then he stopped and looked at me over his shoulder. "I got no reason not to warn you," he said. "No gain either way. Besides, I like you. You were gonna give the urchins some food, even if they were smart enough not to accept. Under the circumstances."

"All I need is information," I called to him. "Can you at least point me to someone who knows where I can find Drizzt?"

"Hells, kid, I know where you can find him. It's the telling you part that isn't going to happen."

"Then point me to someone who will tell me!" I said, throwing up my hands.

THE SHADOWMASK

"Why do you want to find him so bad?" asked the halfling.

"He has something of mine," I lied.

"So that's it then." He sauntered back to me. "Drow stole from you, did he? What'd he take?"

"None of your business, is what," I snapped.

"Hey, you don't share with me, I don't share with you, got it?"

I frowned. I had no reason to trust him, but I had no better options. "I have to talk to him," I mumbled at last. "He has some information I need."

"Oh ho! So you want information about the whereabouts of the guy who's got your information. That's something, ain't it!" Dondon laughed. "Well, sorry, I can't help you then. There's no way you would get close enough to him to talk, that's for sure. If it were, you know, a sack of gold or a magic ring, that'd be one thing. Entreri's a killer, not a mugger. He's not after the loot. I could've maybe helped you get it back, you know what I mean? But information?" He sliced his hands through the air. "No way." With that, he disappeared around the corner.

I waited a few moments. Then I slipped around the corner after him. I had often shadowed Perrault before, and was quite competent at it. The trick, I knew, was not staying hidden, but blending. Of course, there were plenty of tricks to counter shadowing—choke points, sudden direction changes, backtracking, all designed to make obvious the person trying to blend in—but using these methods relied on the knowledge, or at least suspicion, that one was being followed. Which, I hoped, Dondon did not possess.

Dondon walked quickly, moving deftly through the crowded street, very possibly picking a few pockets along the way.

All the squalor that plagued Memnon was abundant in Calimport as well. We passed by makeshift hovels made of shoddy driftwood, leaning against the sides of great mansions. Towering spires looked over broad slums. A horde of beggars flanked the doors of a great temple. And Calimport had a distinctive smell to it: the stench of unwashed bodies covered with far too much rich perfume. It was as if the city's wealthy had tried to hide the odor of the poor.

The longer I followed Dondon, the more certain I was that he had a destination in mind. And given our previous conversation, I figured he was probably heading to Entreri, or someone who knew Entreri, to let him know I had been snooping around.

But would that really be so bad? Dondon and the urchins on the street surely feared Entreri. Drizzt, on the other hand, had never even mentioned him. Though that wasn't the only thing the drow hadn't mentioned to me. He had never told me what he wanted with the stone, either. I had no idea which of Drizzt's words were true and which were false, and no way to determine between the two.

But I needed to find Drizzt. I needed to know why he was after the stone. And I needed to know if he could help me, if we could search for it together.

A great bell in the temple ahead of me began to ring. My eyes darted through the sea of worshippers streaming out of the temple doors, and I cursed. I had lost track of Dondon. I raced up the street, passing row after row of driftwood shacks. As I passed a dark alley, an arm reached out and pulled me in. I couldn't help but let out a yelp.

"I knew you'd follow me, foolish kid," Dondon said, but his voice was not as harsh as his words. He sounded almost impressed.

I leaned against the high stone wall, willing my

racing heart to slow back to normal. "I need to know what I'm up against."

"Of course. Allow me to show you." He pointed down the alley. "The road out there is Rogue's Circle. At the end of the road you'll see a three-story brown storehouse. Outside are four men who look like vagrants."

"Look like, but aren't," I said, beginning to piece the puzzle together.

"Precisely. They're guards. The house belongs to Pasha Pook."

I peered down the alley to try to catch a glimpse of the house or the so-called guards. But all I could see at the end of the alley was a sliver of cobblestoned road lined with iron grates and what looked like a tavern door across the way. I turned back to Dondon. "Who's Pasha Pook?" I asked.

"He's the most powerful man in Calimport, kid," Dondon replied, crossing his arms over his chest. "Even more so since his assassin came home."

"His assassin?"

"Entreri. Most dangerous man in the city."

I let out a frustrated sigh. "You just said Pasha Pook was the most dangerous man in the city."

THE *SHADOWMASK*

"Pook's the most powerful. He can have anyone killed, anytime, for any reason. Don't cross Pook. But Entreri's the most dangerous. He's the one doing the killing."

"Okay. So what's this got to do with Drizzt?"

"The drow crossed Entreri, and the assassin led him here to die. He and his buddies went to Pook's house yesterday, which means they're either dead or captured. If the drow's your friend, hope he's dead. And either way, forget about him." Dondon punched my leg, nearly knocking me down, despite his small size. "This is the last time I tell you to drop it. If you don't, I won't shed a tear when you disappear."

I looked at him long and hard, trying to discern if the concern on his face was real. "You're heading to Entreri right now to tell him everything."

He laughed in my face. "What would I say?" he said when he'd caught his breath. He raised his voice to a mocking high pitch. "Hey, Mister Entreri, sir, there's some little kid from out of town asking about the dark elf. Want that I should kill him for you?" His voice dropped back to normal. "He'd probably kill me for wasting his time!"

Dondon kept laughing as he walked away. I briefly considered running after him, knocking him out, maybe taking him prisoner. Perhaps I could arrange an exchange for Drizzt?

Or perhaps I would simply end up dead. I had enough powerful enemies as it was.

My shoulders sagged, and I sat back against the alley wall. What was I supposed to do? Luck had always been on my side. I had been named for luck; the stone I sought was an artifact of Tymora, the goddess of good fortune herself. And yet Tymora smiled on me no more. I shook my left hand, which had grown completely numb ever since I fought the bandit in the oasis. Pinpricks were creeping up my left foot as well.

I'm just tired, I told myself. I hadn't slept since the previous day, and had run many miles across the desert since that last rest. I needed to find somewhere to sleep. And I knew just the place.

In a sprawling city like Calimport, it would take years for me to learn my way around. But there was one exception, one landmark I could find easily in any city.

Locating the docks was a matter of using my nose, following the breezes carrying the salt of the sea. In Calimport, the docks stretched for miles along the coast, and extended as far as the eye could see onto the water. Some piers had as many as eight ships docked alongside—and not small boats, but huge oceangoing trade ships, four-masted, six-decked monstrosities that put *Sea Sprite* to shame. At the foot of each dock, a lamppost stood over a bubbling fountain. The fountain offered clean water to disembarking sailors—and to the many vagabonds roaming the wharves—and the lamp offered light when night fell.

I walked along the expansive docks for nearly an hour before I found my hiding place: a collection of blackened crates, waiting to be loaded into a warehouse farther down the pier. I was careful to choose a stack that had no activity around it and found a nook in the seaward face of the pile.

One of the crates had cracked open on one side, and through the split wood, I spied slivers of dried, salted meat. My rumbling belly would not listen to any objections about stealing. I ate my fill with no second thoughts.

The sea breeze felt good on my face; the salt smelled like perfume to my nose. The sounds around me all felt so familiar: the gentle lapping of the sea against the base of the docks, and the creaking of the ships as they rose and fell on the tidal swells. Sailors and deckhands and dockmasters shouted commands as they rushed by. They raised sails and lowered them, loaded and unloaded cargo, called out permission to dock, permission to come aboard, "yes Cap'n, no Cap'n."

I wished I could find another ship at the docks and sail away, but I knew that I could no longer run from my troubles.

I steeled my resolve, determined to follow my path to its end. When night fell, I would go to Rogue's Circle. Drizzt and his friends were in danger at the hands of a crazed assassin, and there was a good chance I was the only one who knew it. How I would get past Pook's guards or fight Entreri, for that I had no plan. I would have to improvise. Once I had saved Drizzt, I could question him; perhaps then he'd have no choice but to tell me everything he knew about the stone. I dared to hope that he would be so grateful, he would agree to help me, and we could track down the woman in the mask together.

It was a dangerous plan for sure, but I had come too far to let any setback stop me. Even if it led to my death.

For a long time, I stared at the boats, enjoying the smell of the sea breeze for what I was sure would be the last time. Eventually I drifted off to dreams of sailing on Captain Deudermont's ship, scanning the open sea from the crow's nest with a wheat-haired girl by my side.

"I'm not looking for a job, or for passage, or anything," I said.

"Based on the circumstances of your departure, I didn't expect you were," he replied curtly.

"Yes, sir. But you see—" I cleared my throat. "I need a favor."

How best to say it, I wondered. If I blurted out that Drizzt had been captured by the most dangerous man in Calimport and I needed to get him back, so he could tell me where the stone he never expressed any interest in is, so I could get back that same stone, which I left *Sea Sprite* intending to be rid of as soon as possible, Deudermont would probably give me a funny look, and bid me farewell. At the least.

"Drizzt is in trouble," I began. "He's been captured by dangerous people."

"I knew he sought dangerous people," said Deudermont. "But he is himself dangerous, when he needs to be. Are you sure he is captured?"

"I have it from a good source," I said. But then I reconsidered my only source: Dondon, a halfling posing as a child. A professional liar.

My doubt must have been written across my face. "You are not so sure," the captain said. "But I

Chapter Nine

"What ho, *Sea Sprite*?" The call echoed down the docks.

I rubbed the sleep from my eyes. The sun was low in the western sky, but not yet set. The tide was coming in. I had slept well and long, but still I was weary, and still my hand and foot were numb. I could hardly believe the call I'd heard was anything but a dream, but I couldn't help myself. I had to scan the docks.

And sure enough, there she was, tying off alongside a pier not two hundred yards from my hiding place. It had been less than a tenday since I'd seen her last, but it felt a lifetime ago.

I pulled myself to my feet and walked toward *Sea Sprite*, trying not to put too much weight on my weaker left foot. I could hardly fathom her presence—how, and why, had she come to Calimport?

I had trekked across the desert, had nearly died of thirst, had nearly been killed by bandits. I could have simply stayed with *Sea Sprite* and reached the same place at the same time!

I thought of the reasons I had left the ship: the pirate attack, the troll, the danger my presence brought. My intentions had been honorable when I abandoned *Sea Sprite*. Could I really bring her crew back into all of that? How selfish was I?

No, not selfish. It was not just my fate that hung in the balance. Many more lives than mine were at stake.

I reached the pier where *Sea Sprite* sat docked, to find two familiar faces at the end of the deck.

"Oi, it's Lucky-Twice!" said Lucky. "How'd you get 'ere? Stow away on another boat, then? We'd've given you a ride if we knew you was heading here to Calimport, you know."

Tonnid laughed along with Lucky, but he seemed less sure about the joke.

"I walked," I said. My throat choked up a bit: Lucky and Tonnid had been the closest thing I'd had to friends on the ship. I had thought I would never see them again.

"You walked. From Memnon?"

"Well, ran, really." I shrugged. "Most of the w Walked some of it."

"Sure, kid, and I'm a Lord of Waterdeep." L scoffed and rolled his eyes. "Ain't that right, Tin

Tonnid's laugh turned into a great, uproa cackle. Quickly every head on the pier—and for s piers in each direction—stared at us.

I shielded my face from their stares and s closer to the ship. "Listen, Lucky. Can I come a I need to speak with Captain Deudermont."

"You don't need to come aboard to sp me," said the captain, as he marched across "I had planned to look in on you once we re Memnon, a few tendays from now. I did you to beat me to Calimport."

"Nor did I expect to come, sir," I sai I am."

"Indeed. What can I do for you, the mont asked as he ambled down the gang

will trust your judgment. Who holds him?"

"Pasha Pook."

Deudermont winced at the name. "I have no desire to fight a man as powerful as Pook," he said.

I nodded. "I didn't really expect you to. But thank you anyway." The words tasted bitter in my mouth. I had in fact expected Deudermont would help. He was after all, a noble man. But I couldn't blame him for not wanting to get mixed up in my troubles. I began to walk away.

"Hold up there, Maimun," he said. "I said I have no desire to fight him. But there are other ways to get things done in a city such as this."

I turned back. "What do you mean?" I asked.

"I am fairly prominent among the merchant sailors, and I am connected to Waterdeep. I have some political power at my disposal. Political pressure can be a great tool."

Suddenly things didn't look so bleak. "Can we go right now?" I walked backward to the city, eager to get moving immediately.

I was sure Deudermont would feel the same way. He wouldn't want to see Drizzt and his friends held, and likely tortured, any longer than necessary.

But Deudermont only took one step onto the dock, then stopped.

I motioned him forward. "Come on! You never know how long it could take for you to apply pressure, or whatever. If we want to rescue Drizzt from Pasha Pook, we have to go right now!"

Deudermont just smiled, even laughed a bit, as he looked right past me.

I turned to see what he was looking at and walked directly into the lamppost behind me.

I bounced back and rubbed my head. Only then did I realize it was no lamppost, but a leg. A leg attached to a tall flaxen-haired barbarian.

"Wulfgar!" I shouted.

"Sounds like you've got a solid plan there, Maimun," said Wulfgar. On one of his shoulders rested a massive warhammer. The bicep of his other arm was wrapped in a clean white linen bandage. "So whom are we pressuring? I am a fair hand at applying pressure myself, you know." He swung the hammer down from his shoulder, slapping it into his palm. He winced slightly at the impact.

"Yeah, like ye pressured that hydra into not eating ye," said a rough and gruff voice behind the barbarian. The red-bearded dwarf, Bruenor, shambled into view. Had he been hiding behind Wulfgar deliberately? His axe was belted at his hip, his shield was slung over his back, and his one-horned helm sat crooked on his head. "Ye only let him take the one bite!"

He reached up to slap Wulfgar's wounded arm, but the barbarian simply raised his elbow a bit, and the dwarf could not reach his target. Bruenor settled for a sharp punch to the barbarian's side instead. Wulfgar hardly seemed to notice.

Beside him stood Catti-brie, the woman who had held my hand on *Sea Sprite* many tendays before. My hand moved to my chest instinctively, to the black mark where my wound had been tarred over. Seeing Catti-brie made the scar ache once more, but the sight of her auburn hair blowing in the sea breeze was worth the pain.

"Ye're not one for subtlety," said Catti-brie to Bruenor. Her voice carried the same accent as the dwarf, but sounded far sweeter. "Ye'd rather kick down the front door."

"Hey! The door I kicked down was in the sewers, remember?" Bruenor said.

"It was a thieves' guild," said a voice from nearby. It took me a moment to locate its source: the rooftop of the warehouse beside the pier. "The sewer door is the front door."

I took in a sharp breath.

He was wearing his magical mask again, I realized, which made him look like a surface elf. But his violet eyes could not be hidden. I scanned his face, my stomach roiling, terrified he would greet me as a foe, not a friend. But he seemed happy to see me. "Come on," Drizzt called out. "Are we going to go to Pasha Pook's house to rescue me, or not?"

"You mean Pasha Regis's house," Wulfgar said. They all burst into laughter. Even though I didn't understand the joke, I laughed too, grateful for a reason to smile again.

"All right, enough of this," said Captain Deudermont from behind me. "There is some storytelling to do, and I think this story will be enjoyed best in the privacy of my cabin." He turned and walked back up the gangplank. The four adventurers followed, still laughing.

A new energy lightened my step. It would not be long before I had the information I needed.

But when I reached the gangplank, Captain Deudermont held up his hand. "You are welcome aboard my ship," he said to me. "But I will speak with these four in private first. I expect that you will not eavesdrop."

I started to object, but Deudermont's look was so harsh and unbending that I thought the better of it. "Of course not, sir," I mumbled.

"Good. I will speak to you when I have finished with them," Deudermont said. Without another word he led Drizzt, Wulfgar, Catti-brie, and Bruenor onto and across the deck and into his cabin. I slunk up the gangplank a few moments later and onto the deck.

We were in port, and night was falling. I looked up at the mainmast. There was no lookout posted in the crow's nest.

Soon I would confront Drizzt and demand answers. I would very likely have to leave the ship, and my friends, once more. But before that, I would sleep in the crow's nest underneath the stars. I would be exactly where I wished to be.

CHAPTER TEN

The sound of someone climbing the ladder broke my trance perhaps an hour later, just as the last rays of light disappeared beneath the horizon. I pulled out my dagger, ready to strike.

"The captain said you were looking for me," Drizzt said, pulling himself gracefully into the broad bucket beside me.

"I was." I put my dagger back in my belt, but kept my hand on the hilt.

"For what purpose?"

"I . . . I need to know something." I hung my head. All the time I had been searching for the drow, I had never really imagined what I would say once I finally found him. I knew Drizzt was a formidable fighter. What if my questions made him angry? I gulped. Fear weighed down my voice. My question came out at barely a whisper. "What do you want with my stone?"

"What stone?" He looked genuinely puzzled.

"The magical stone. The stone I carried in a pouch here," I said, tapping the hollow of my chest. How could he pretend to not know what I was talking about? My voice grew stronger. "I had it last time we were on this ship. I nearly tossed it away the night we met, when you found me on deck. I'm sure you knew about it then, didn't you?" I said, though in fact I was not at all sure.

But Drizzt did not deny it. "And you have lost it now," he said.

"Not lost—it was stolen!" I practically spat out the words. "It was stolen by a woman. She wears a shadow-mask and a robe, and the ravens said she was trying to save me and—"

"Ravens?" Drizzt interrupted.

"Talking ravens," I said. "Nine of them. Or, one of them talked, I don't know about the rest."

"Where is your stone now?" Drizzt asked.

"That's what I'm asking you." I was growing desperate. "Where is it? I have to get it back, and I thought since you were after it too, you would know!"

"I am not after your stone, Maimun." Drizzt looked down at me, with no menace in his eyes. "Why would you think I was?"

"I met a seer in Memnon." The words sounded foolish to my own ears, and a blush crept over my cheeks. "He told me you seek what I seek." Had the old seer lied to me? A feeling like hot needles shot through my left leg.

Drizzt shook his head slowly. "All I seek right now is passage back to the north, to help my friend recover his home. I know nothing of any such stone."

My heart sank. I clenched my fist, trying in vain to relieve the pinpricks shooting up and down my arm as well.

"What is the matter? Are you in pain?" Drizzt said, pointing at my hand.

"No," I said. I tried to blink back the tears in my eyes and look normal.

He ignored my obvious lie. "You are wounded."

"It's nothing." I stared at my hand and wiggled my fingers. "My hand just feels a little numb."

"Just your hand?"

My gaze dropped to the bucket's worn floor. "My left foot too," I admitted.

"Since when?" There was genuine concern in his voice and on his face, and I felt ashamed for ever having doubted his motives.

"Since . . . Since I left *Sea Sprite*, I suppose," I tried to think back to exactly when the feeling had started, to what had caused it. "No, since I lost the stone. It's powerful magic, brings luck and stuff. And it's been mine since birth even though I only got it this summer, and it's tied to me somehow and . . ." My voice rose in speed and intensity as I rambled on frantically.

Drizzt patted the air and motioned for me to be calm. "I know little of any of this," he said. "But it sounds to me like the numbness and the stone are connected." He squatted down and reached out to touch my leg. I jerked it back reflexively.

Drizzt looked back at me, deep concern in his eyes. "You must find your stone, or I cannot say how much worse this pain and numbness might grow."

I took a few deep breaths until the pinpricks began to subside. "Can you help me?"

R.A. & GENO SALVATORE

"I will do what I can, but I fear that is not much."

I dropped my head.

"But," the drow continued, "I do know of someone who may be able to help."

I looked up again. "Who?" I asked.

"A man, a wizard, named Malchor Harpell. He lives to the north, in a hidden tower. I can take you there, if you will trust me."

My head swirled with hope. I had a destination, a place to begin again. I nodded.

"Good," Drizzt rose to his feet and headed for the ladder. "Now, the captain is waiting for you in his cabin."

Part Two

THE SHADOWMASK

"So ye went down to the cabin and ye spilled yer beans to Captain Deudermont," the pirate said. He sat on a boulder in front of me, his elbows perched on his knees, his head resting in one hand.

"That's right," I said. I cast my gaze behind the pirate. I could see that the light coming through the door had changed significantly. It no longer came through the door so directly. But a faint glow still seeped through the cracks. It was indirect sunlight pouring into the tunnel that led to the beach. I would not have even noticed it, except that I had been watching for it, waiting for the answers it would bring.

The sun was rising, not setting.

The cave faced east.

"So then ye sailed north," the pirate chanted. "And ye found this Harpell person, and—"

"If you want to tell the story, be my guest," I snapped.

"A story that boring? Why'd I want to tell it?"

"Why would you want to hear it, is the better question."

The pirate laughed and pulled himself to his feet. "Good question, that be," he said, hand going for the hilt of his sword.

He brought the sword up and advanced menacingly.

"You don't want to kill me," I said.

"Not if ye got more to say," he said. "And if it ain't boring."

I made no response, just locked my gaze with his. After a moment, he sat back down. "So, ye talked Deudermont into taking yerself north, then."

"He volunteered, actually," I replied. "For the second time, he offered me his help unconditionally."

"So long as ye give in to his will."

"That's right."

The pirate leaned forward. "Pretty strong condition, that be."

"Are you going to stop interrupting me?"

He laughed again, a great belly laugh that rolled for what seemed like several minutes.

"I'll take that as a no," I said when he'd finished.

"I be a pirate, boy! We ain't known fer politeness."

"Nor for bathing either," I said, unable to resist.

"Nor that," he agreed. "Now, do continue with the tale. There be a long way between Calimport and Waterdeep."

A big part of me wanted to simply stop talking, to let him kill me, to deny him the pleasure of knowing the end of my tale. But I could not do that, not after what I had learned.

The cave faced east.

It faced open water.

That meant we were on an island, somewhere off the Sword Coast.

That meant the pirates would have ships, boats, some means of reaching the mainland, near at hand.

The beginnings of a plan formed in my mind. A desperate plan, true, but a plan nonetheless.

I could not let this pirate kill me. After everything I'd been through, I would not be killed like an aging animal too old to serve its purpose. But for the moment, I had no choice but to give the pirate what he wanted, until the time was right to make my escape.

CHAPTER ELEVEN

"Sails on the horizon! South by southwest!" I called down from my perch in the crow's nest. We had been at sea for seventeen days, harnessing a strong autumnal wind blowing from the south to push us up the Sword Coast at a good clip. Autumn was dragging on toward winter, and the ice floes and icebergs of the northern seas would soon begin creeping down toward Waterdeep. We had passed Memnon more than a tenday ago. We were but a few days from Baldur's Gate, where we planned to make port and take in more supplies. I almost wished we'd never get there.

I had been there twice before, both times ending worse than my worst nightmares. I had battled Asbeel there, had watched Perrault take a grievous wound defending me, and had abandoned him to die there. I would surely have died there myself, had I not found *Sea Sprite*. And back aboard her again, I felt like I had come home.

After we departed Calimport, Deudermont assigned me the job of carrying his orders, the same job I had held before taking my sudden leave in Memnon. As the numbness in my left foot grew worse, it became more and more difficult to walk. In spite of the pain, I was willing to continue my duties without complaint, but Captain Deudermont would hear nothing of it. He said I had eyes as sharp as any on the ship, and could make better account of myself as lookout.

"Sails on the horizon!" I called out again. The season was late, so we saw relatively few ships, and nearly all of those sailed from the north to Calimshan. "She's tracing the horizon," I called down. "Looks like she's heading for land."

Odd, I thought. The coastline nearest us was Tyr, its purple hills meeting the sea at rocky and often sheer cliffs. There were few, if any, good berths due east of that ship's position.

We were faster than her, but her angle would bring her closer to us as she passed directly south of our due-north track. Her choice of path was curious, surely, but something else was amiss. I couldn't quite place it. I watched her move ever so slowly across my field of vision, away from the darkening western horizon . . .

The darkening western horizon. Darkening, in the early afternoon. Suddenly the ship was the least of my concerns.

"Captain!" I yelled down to the deck below. "I need the captain!" A boy named Waillan, who had taken over my duties as deckhand, darted below deck and emerged a moment later with Captain Deudermont in tow.

"What is it?" Deudermont called up. Even yelling, his voice sounded regal.

"Ship south-southwest, moving due east," I called down. "I think she's damaged, looks to be listing."

Deudermont nodded. "Heading for Tyr, for repairs," he said.

"No sir, I don't think she's on course for any city. She's just aiming for the nearest land."

"Any thoughts on why?"

"I think she's running from a storm," I yelled, more loudly than I had planned.

A hush fell over all the crew on deck. A storm so late in the season likely meant a tempest. A tempest could make a ship like ours disappear.

"You think?" Deudermont said. "Look again and tell me if there is a storm or if there is not."

All work on deck halted. All eyes turned to look at me.

I turned back to the horizon and peered out, squinting my eyes to cut through the glare of the high sun. And again I saw it: the western horizon growing dark, dimmed by the approaching thunderhead. The clouds would be visible in a matter of hours, I knew. And a few hours after that, we would be in the thick of it.

"Storm," I called down. "Huge, too. Covers the whole western horizon."

Deudermont nodded and looked me straight in the eye. Then he moved to the port stern to scan the horizon himself. I felt a twinge of bitterness that the captain hadn't trusted my eyes.

"Sails to full!" he called after only a moment. "Get all hands on deck! Tie down the cargo, close the portholes, and make the ship ready! We'll run 'til we're caught, then ride it out!" The crew leaped into action immediately. "Helm, set us bearing zero-four-zero. Head toward land until the coast is in sight. We'll need the reference to reach the Gate in a storm."

"Aye," called the helmsman, turning the wheel to the right. Though it was only a slight movement, up in the crow's nest, I felt the boat tilt distinctly.

I glanced out at the listing ship. "Wait! No!" I called down.

But with all the hustle and bustle on deck, Deudermont could not hear me. Men climbed the rigging to open the sails. Others scrambled about with ropes to tie down and brace all the various moving parts on deck. A constant stream of activity entered and left the hold.

"Relief!" I called down below. There should have been someone ready to take my place whenever I conceded the watch. But Deudermont's new orders had trumped that plan. My appointed reliever was busily battening down a hatch somewhere.

I scanned the deck. "Relief! If you please!"

Still no one heard me. At the front of the deck, I saw Wulfgar pulling up the anchor chain—the entire anchor—over the side of the ship, along with a few other crewmen. If the anchor were allowed to hang, as it usually did, and the storm damaged that part of the ship, the anchor could drop into the sea and be lost. Or worse, it could drop into the sea but not be lost, instead catching something on the seabed below and holding us in position. Not being able to rise and fall and move with the swells of the storm could cause catastrophic damage.

Bruenor leaned over the rail, bidding a fond farewell to his lunch for the seventeenth straight day.

Drizzt was walking in the rigging, moving with ease and grace beyond anything I'd seen. He walked along the narrow beams and ropes as if they were solid ground. He was busy helping unfurl the last of the sails, bringing us from half to full. The sight made me a bit nervous. If our sails were out fully when the storm caught us, they'd be ripped to shreds. Deudermont was betting the extra distance we'd cover in the run before the storm would be worth the risk. He would order all sails furled and secured before the front of the tempest hit us.

"I've got ye," came a call from below, a female voice. I knew without looking it was Catti-brie, the only woman on the ship.

I slid down the mast. I had become quite good at dropping from the crow's nest to the deck. She climbed up, offering me a wink as she passed.

As soon as I reached the deck, I set off in a limping sprint, straight to the captain.

"Sir, you missed something," I tried to keep the trepidation out of my voice.

"What's that, Maimun?" Deudermont replied curtly. He did not take his eyes off the horizon, which visibly darkened even from our low perch.

"The other ship."

"What about her?"

"She's listing, sir, and I think she's damaged. We have to help her." Visions of the last ship I hadn't helped flashed in my mind, visions of Joen in chains . . . "We can get to her before the storm does if we turn and set full," I said.

Deudermont turned to face me. "We'd be sailing straight into the wind."

"No, sir, you're wrong," I pointed toward the thundercloud. "See, the storm is coming from the west; it should push the wind in front of it. The storm is probably cycloning, spinning, so the wind will come in from the southwest. If we set to intercept the ship, we'll be headed southeast. The wind won't be perfect, but we can still ride it."

He stared down at me. "Then we'd both be caught in the storm."

"We're going to be caught in the storm anyway," I said, stepping up on the bottom edge of the rail to meet his gaze. "She's already listing, Captain."

"And unlikely to survive the storm. Our presence near her won't change that," Deudermont said. He turned back to the rail, indicating the end of the conversation.

I tugged on his sleeve, willing him to turn back around. "We can take her crew on board, shelter them," I said, fully aware of my own rudeness.

Deudermont continued to stare at the horizon. "I will not risk my own ship and the lives of my crew. Thank you for your opinion, but my decision is made."

I stomped my foot. "Your decision is wrong, sir," I said.

Deudermont whirled back to face me, a fire in his eyes I had never seen. "I am captain of this ship, not you. I am charged with making these decisions, not you. And do not think you are the only one who can see clearly here. I know what is likely to happen, I have weighed all my options, and I have made my choice. When you have an opinion to voice, I will hear it, but once my decision is made, you will not question it so long as you remain on my ship. Am I clear?"

"Yes, sir," I mumbled.

"Good. You are relieved from duty." Without another word, Deudermont stomped away from me toward the stern.

I could barely breathe, let alone speak, as I watched him walk away. I limped to the hold. Belowdecks, I found the hammock that served as my bunk, and fell into it. But I was too humiliated to sleep. Deudermont had just relieved me during an all-hands situation. Never before had he done such a thing to any of his sailors. I could hardly fathom an insult of that magnitude. I flexed my numb hand, and felt the pinpricks traveling up my forearm. Had the other crew heard the discussion—the fight? Would Captain Deudermont tell them how insolent I'd been? I turned my head to my pillow. I'd never be able to show my face abovedecks again.

"The storm's turned," said a voice—Tonnid's voice, low and slow and steady. "Cap'n said you should know."

"Turned south?" I asked, rubbing sleep from my eyes.

"Nopers. Turned north."

I sat up. "Running alongside us?"

"Yepper, just a few miles to our'n west. She's giving us a good wind too, right in our backs! Like a big guy blowing on us!" He puffed up his cheeks and blew a puff of air—and a mouthful of spit—right at me.

I wiped my cheek. He blushed bright red, and offered a small apologetic giggle.

But I was hardly concerned with a little spittle. "What of the other ship? Did the storm catch her?"

"Nope, turned before it got to her. We all had a good cheer on deck."

I smiled. "Thanks, Tonnid. That makes me feel a lot better."

"Good, 'cause the Cap'n said if you feel better you should come back up on deck." He laughed a little. "Never knew you to get seasick, Lucky Lucky." He turned and walked away.

Seasick? Captain Deudermont had told Tonnid I was seasick? I felt my anger at the captain disappear.

I vowed never to cross him again. I tugged on my boots—my ordinary leather boots. Waillan had outgrown them, so he'd passed them on to me. I still had Sali Dalib's boots of course, but I kept them tucked away with the rest of my things in a canvas pack. They were hardly suitable for life aboard a ship.

I raced back abovedecks. The storm was just off our port side, due west of us. That is to say, sheets of rain were just a few miles off our side, clearly visible. Where we were, the sky was overcast, and the wind was howling, sweeping up directly from the south. The sails had been reduced to half—the wind was so strong it would've ripped our rigging apart if the sails were up. But still we moved at an incredible clip.

Up in the rigging, a few of the more agile crew, including Drizzt, held position, waiting for the call to stow the remaining sails. The decision would have to be made fast if the storm turned. Even a slight change would have it atop us in a matter of minutes. Cattibrie was still up in the crow's nest, and when she saw me emerge from below she waved and beckoned me to join her.

"Won't be long now 'til we reach the Gate," Cattie-brie said. "Perhaps the captain will give ye leave for a few hours and ye can visit with some o' yer old friends?"

My friends. Though Catti-brie had meant to comfort me, my stomach flipped at the thought.

There were two people in Baldur's Gate whom I could call friends. Alviss, Perrault's dwarf wizard friend, had used his magic to help me spy on Perrault before. Like the seer in Memnon, he could probably try to peer through that crystal ball of his, to locate the stone, to help me if I asked.

And then there was Jaide: the beautiful elf, the priestess of Tymora. She surely could help me, and just as surely would offer her assistance should I ask.

But I did not dare to ask. To find Jaide, I would need to speak to Alviss. And to find Alviss, I would have to visit his inn, the Empty Flagon. The Empty Flagon where I had delivered Perrault, just before he died. I shuddered. I never wanted to see that place again.

Malchor Harpell, I told myself, was all the help I would need. We'd be in Waterdeep in a tenday, and at his Tower of Twilight before winter made the land impassable. Until then, I would not leave *Sea Sprite*, where I could pretend to be an ordinary sailor, relieved for just a little while of the burden of the stone.

I spent the last few hours of that day watc
curious behavior of the storm from my high
point, praying it would push us off course a
our arrival. But when I rose in the morn
storm's steady wind stayed behind us, drivir
faster toward Baldur's Gate.

Chapter Twelve

The storm did eventually turn east and overtake us a day and a half later, just as we sailed up the Chionthar and made port at Baldur's Gate. Our initial plan had us stopping in the Gate for merely one day to resupply. But the storm had other ideas. It sat over Baldur's Gate, hardly moving, keeping us locked in. The first day was agony for me. I waited belowdecks, avoiding the sight of the docks. I was afraid of the memories they would bring back, mostly. But I was also certain Asbeel would be there, watching, waiting for me.

On the second day, with the ship supplied but the storm not breaking, Captain Deudermont gave shore leave to any of the crew who desired it. Lucky and Tin tried to get me to go to a tavern with them, but I pretended the captain had given me work to do. I fell asleep that night, praying for the storm to end. I tossed and turned, my sleep torn apart with nightmares about Asbeel.

The next morning, I crawled abovedecks, certain I would see blue sky. But still the rain poured down in sheets. Through the low clouds, I thought I saw a dark plume lazily rising from the city. I climbed up to the crow's nest to see where it was coming from. The outer district? My stomach clenched.

Without thinking, ignoring all my previous reasoning, I rushed down the gangplank and into Baldur's Gate, limping along as quickly as I could. I had only been in the city twice, but somehow I had memorized the route. After only a few minutes I rounded a corner to see the familiar sign, the single mug, drained of liquid: The Empty Flagon.

The building was ablaze, and a small crowd had gathered to watch as the flames leaped high into the air in defiance of the torrential rain, sometimes accentuated by a pop or a hiss or a small explosion. The buildings beside the inn were pressed tight against it, as were most structures in the city, but the flame didn't seem interested in them, barely licked against their wet wooden walls.

I moved to the crowd of bystanders, asking quietly if anyone knew what was going on.

"Dunno, really," one man said. "Place just lit up like a candle. No warning, didn't see no one there."

"What about the owner?" I asked.

"The dwarf? He ain't been around in o'er a tenday. Just up and disappeared one day, and the people stopped coming."

"Actually been nice, not having them ruffians coming through all the time," a woman nearby said. "Got nothing against dwarves, you know? But they like to drink, and drunk people always want to fight, you know?"

"Anyone know where Alviss went? The owner?" I asked.

"He didn't tell no one, didn't pack up and move or anything," said the first man. "Just up and vanished, like I said."

I started back to the docks, then thought better of it. Something odd was going on, and I had a feeling a certain demon was behind it. And if he'd gone after

Alviss, he may have gone after another one of our friends . . .

I could hardly manage a run, with my left leg numb from the knee down, but I went as quickly as I could to the temple district and the great Temple of Tymora.

The massive structure was imposing indeed, even more so in the downpour. Its gargoyles leered out menacingly through the rain, and its smooth walls glistened as if possessed by some inner light. I considered going around the back of the building, to where I knew there would be a door. But I did not have the password, so instead I ventured through the main entrance.

The nave of the main temple was huge, lined with tapestries depicting Tymora and her legendary heroes, sometimes in battle but more often simply in some heroic pose. Huge marble columns lined the nave, with yet more tapestries strung between them, dividing the structure into three paths.

Down the center aisle, before the altar, a young man in white robes holding an armful of candles approached one of the tapestries.

I moved swiftly toward him, taking note of his

jet-black hair, his slightly pointed ears, his angular face. He was half elf, I was sure.

"Excuse me," I said. "I was wondering if you could help me."

"I am quite busy, but I'm sure one of the disciples will aid you," the half-elf priest replied. He arranged his candles—seven of them, long of neck and longer of wick—side by side under the center of the tapestry. The tapestry depicted Tymora in a white robe holding a lit candle, standing side by side with her twin sister, Beshaba, goddess of misfortune, wearing black and holding an unlit candle. The priest lit the wick of the candle closest to Tymora's side of the tapestry, and knelt before them.

"What are you doing?" I asked. I knew I was being rude, but I couldn't help myself.

"I am praying for one of our lost sisters," he said in a nasal voice. "That Tymora will guide her home. Now leave me to my prayers, child." He began whispering under his breath. As I watched, the wick of the lit candle fell sidelong onto the next, and after a moment the second candle was alight.

"It will only take a moment. I just need to speak with Jaide."

"I said—" The priest's words caught in his throat, and he rose suddenly, spinning to face me, and nearly lighting his white robe on fire with the candles. "How do you know that name?" he whispered harshly.

"She is a friend. And I need to find her."

He studied me up and down and looked at my face, at my tunic—at my cloak. His eyes widened with surprise and what I thought might be horror. "You are Perrault's ward," he said, still whispering.

Behind him, the second candle fell into the third, and that one caught fire as well.

"Yes," I said, "I was Perrault's ward. And now I need help. So tell me where Jaide is."

"She left a tenday ago. It is for her that I pray." He sounded somewhat angry. "But there is someone who needs to see you. Please, wait here." He motioned to a disciple, then disappeared through a well-concealed door behind the altar. The disciple came over to the tapestry, bowed to me, and knelt before the tapestry, apparently to continue the priest's prayer. The third candle, in the meantime, dipped into the fourth.

I motioned to the line of candles. "What is that?" I asked.

"A prayer to Tymora," said the disciple. "The candles can fall either toward or away from the next in line. Tymora guides them, to tell us whether luck will be good or ill for that which we pray about."

"So the more candles are lit, the better the luck?"

"Not quite. Misfortune is often just good fortune taken too far, so teaches Tymora. The best position for the candles is the fourth, where the fire is now. But any farther"—as he said it, the fourth candle dipped into the fifth, which then fell onto the sixth, and that into the seventh, in rapid succession—"and the luck is ill. Oh, this is not good. I must pray for our sister, please. Wait at the altar for Priest Aridren to return." The disciple pushed through the door behind the altar. Through the dark crack, I thought I saw a flash of red skin.

I leaped off the altar, sprinting as far and as fast as my lame leg would carry me, all the way back to *Sea Sprite*.

I knew whom Priest Aridren had gone to fetch. I did not wish to be there when Asbeel emerged from that door.

The storm did not break for another thirteen days, during which neither hide nor hair of me could be seen anywhere but belowdecks on *Sea Sprite*. I spent much of my time those days playing a card game called *Three Dragon Ante* with Lucky and Tonnid. Tonnid, despite his generally slow mind, turned out to be quite good at odds. We did not bet money, but rather duties and chores, and by the time the storm finally broke and the sun came out, I owned most of Tonnid's turns cleaning the bilges, or clearing the galley after meals, or aiding the galley cook, or any other unpleasant task he had wanted to be rid of, all the way to Waterdeep.

It would be a long journey. But at least I would not have much idle time. Any time not spent doing something would find my mind wandering to Asbeel and Priest Aridren, whom I was convinced was his servant; to the stone, and the uncertainty I had surrounding it; or back in time, to Perrault, Alviss, Jaide, and Elbeth, all of whom had tried to protect me and suffered instead.

A cooperative wind could've gotten us to Waterdeep inside ten days. But on the fourth day out of Baldur's Gate, the biting north wind blew in, trying to drive us back to fairer waters.

The northern breeze more than doubled the time of our journey. During the day, we would have to tack into the wind, slowing us greatly. At night, we could not sail, for fear of colliding with the icebergs from the Sea of Moving Ice far to the north.

I hoped the wind would break, but the more experienced sailors all knew that was impossible. Once the wind had turned, it would not shift again until the spring. We would have to cut through it if we meant to reach Waterdeep.

The farther north we sailed, the slower the going became. On the eleventh day, the fears of an iceberg proved true, and though it appeared by daylight, we had to tack off course to avoid the massive, deadly chunk of ice.

From that evening on, all sails were firmly stored each night, the anchor dropped, and the launch's beacon was lit. The small craft rowed a few hundred yards out ahead of the ship each night with two men assigned to it, tasked with staying awake and watching for dangerous ice.

I drew that duty once, and it was among the worst nights of my life. The temperature dipped far lower than I thought possible—it was late autumn, not winter!—and the breeze bit through even Perrault's magical cloak. By the time dawn broke and we rowed back to *Sea Sprite*, my teeth were chattering so badly I feared my jaw would rattle right off my face.

But something else happened that night, something that gave me hope. For in spite of that terrible cold, my left hand held fast to the oars. There on that freezing little boat, I realized that the colder it got, and the closer we got to Waterdeep, the less numbness and pain I felt. From that day on, my condition, though not cured, did not grow any worse. I knew not what it meant, but after that night, my nightmares ceased, and I no longer hoped to stay aboard *Sea Sprite* forever. I couldn't wait to reach the Tower of Twilight, where Malchor Harpell could give me answers and I could begin my journey anew.

CHAPTER THIRTEEN

The captain had taken the helm himself the last few days, and as we sailed around the last bend into Waterdeep Harbor, I saw why. The entirety of the harbor was choked by ice floes large and small, with hardly space between them for a ship. The captain masterfully guided *Sea Sprite*, with Wulfgar pulling the guide ropes as mightily as any man could. The captain's great skill and the barbarian's great strength worked so well in concert I felt as though I were watching a dance. *Sea Sprite's* movements through the choked harbor, missing ice on each side by mere feet, were as graceful as any waltz.

When at last we pulled up to the pier, the stunned expressions of the harbormen, busy breaking down the last of the dock equipment for storage for the winter, were a sight worth seeing.

Soon, they had the pier cleared and ropes ready as we pulled alongside to a chorus of cheers.

Captain Deudermont moved to the rail. "Permission to come ashore, Harbormaster?" he called down.

"Granted, with pleasure, Captain Deudermont!" a man called back, and a second round of cheers went up. "We had hoped you would reach the city before winter locked you out."

"You had hoped?" Deudermont repeated.

"Oh, yes. You are summoned to a council of the Lords, good captain. I believe they've an offer to make you. This very evening, in fact."

Deudermont gave a quick set of orders, and his well-trained crew sprang into action. A group began hauling the trade cargo from the hold, while another began taking on foodstuffs and essential supplies. The sails were furled, all but the main were taken down and stowed; everything loose on the deck found its place for storage. I had not witnessed that particular dance before, but I could surmise its meaning: *Sea Sprite* was making ready for a winter in port.

As if to accentuate my thoughts, a light snow began to fall. Big, wet flakes whirled and spun through the air on the sea breeze, before finally melting into spots of water on the ground. I doubted the snow would stick at all, doubted it would even leave a coat of fresh powder anywhere on the city. But it did signal things to come.

Winter had arrived.

Which meant Drizzt and his companions would wish to be out of the city and on their way. And I with them.

I had next to nothing to pack—just the small sack I kept near my hammock—so instead I leaned on the forward rail and watched the snow fall on Waterdeep, watched the dockworkers at their tasks, watched the girl with the short yellow hair walk past.

My eyes stopped roving and fixed upon her. Despite the cut of her hair, I knew her instantly. I had seen her in my dreams, and until then, I had not imagined that she was still alive, had not imagined anything of her past her disappearance into the hold of that pirate ship.

I could hardly breathe as I limped across the deck, down the gangplank, toward Tonnid standing guard at the end of the pier.

"Hey, Maimun, you ain't got shore leave," Tonnid said, stepping in my way.

"Yeah I do, Tin," I said. "Captain just gave me leave."

"But he ain't even on the ship."

"He left me a note."

Tonnid blinked a few times, stared up as if seeking answers from on high, then finally nodded and stepped aside.

I felt bad for tricking him, until I remembered how many times I'd had to take his shift cleaning out the bilges on the trip from Baldur's Gate to Waterdeep. It served him right, I decided.

But I had more pressing business. Joen was nearly out of sight, her short stature making her difficult to see in a crowd. But I was determined not to lose her. I sprinted off, as fast as I'd managed to run since the desert.

Waterdeep was a northern city, and I was thankful for it. In the south, in Memnon and Calimport, any patch of land without a structure was fair game for erecting a hovel. As such, the roads were unpredict-able, winding, often coming to dead ends suddenly and forcing long backtracks. In the north, in both Baldur's Gate and Waterdeep, the streets were clearly marked (in the better districts, cobbled stone and not dirt), and they followed a somewhat logical order.

Many times over the next hour, I lost sight of Joen as she rounded a corner. But each time, when I rounded the same corner, I could either see her, or see exactly which roads she had taken. Had we been in the South, I surely would have lost her, and been lost and confused myself. But in Waterdeep, I managed to track her all the way through town, until I saw her enter a run-down inn near the middle of the city.

The inn was in such a state of disrepair, I was sur-prised it was even open. A sign hung above the door, but one of the ropes holding it in place had snapped, leaving the shingle dangling awkwardly. The picture on the sign was that of a simple wooden dagger; the faded letters below it spelled out one word: "Shank." A fitting name for such a place, I decided; anyone entering was surely at risk of being stabbed.

I crept up to the inn's door. It stood slightly ajar, and flickering light and plenty of raucous noise came out of it. I glanced behind me. The street looked abandoned, so I peered through the door's crack without fear that someone outside would see me.

Three dozen men and women, one dwarf, and one female halfling stood or sat within. They each held a mug of frothy ale—several people held two. They sat in a semi-circle, all talking with each other, but staring at a figure in the middle. He sat there, his head down and obscured by a great wide-brimmed violet hat, his frame clothed in fine silk of royal purple. Nowhere in the inn did I see Joen. Had I just imagined her after all? The concern fled from me as soon as the figure in the center raised his head.

His face was the blue of the southern seas, his hair the white of ocean spray. I had seen his face before, seen his cold eyes staring at me, felt his mighty grip as he pulled me beneath the water. My hand dropped to my dagger. I gripped the edge of the door tighter, but still I did not dare enter.

"Greetings," the blue pirate said, his voice sweet yet flat. "I am Captain Chrysaor, and you all are now my crew." A murmur went up through the crowd. I blinked. That was highly unusual. It was the crew's choice to sign on with the captain, not the other way around.

Chrysaor held up his hands, signaling for the murmur to die down, then continued. "That you have shown up here tells me you seek gainful employ. And I promise you, in my employ you shall find only the greatest gain."

"What sort of gain?" someone from the crowd called out. By the rough voice, I thought it must've been the dwarf, but then again all those people were pirates, so I couldn't be sure.

"Gold and silver, gems and jewels. A veritable dragon's hoard." Chrysaor replied. "A fortune to be split evenly among all of you. I won't even be taking a share; I want only one artifact from the entire take."

Each person inside apparently decided that was his cue to strike up conversation. The noise level went from a patient silence to a deafening roar instantly.

But I still heard the whisper in my ear with perfect clarity. I felt the sharp edge of the dagger resting against the side of my neck.

"You should not have come here," Joen whispered. She placed her strong hand on my shoulder and pulled me around to face her. I smiled at her, my heart racing. But she did not take the dagger from my neck.

I wanted to tell her everything, everything I'd been through up until the moment that I saw her on the docks. But I couldn't push the words past the lump in my throat. So I settled for a simple question: "Why are you here?"

"You heard him. Gainful employ."

"But you're a sailor, not a pirate." I felt foolish even as the words left my mouth.

She scoffed. "I was a sailor, before my ship was taken by pirates," she said. Her voice was full of venom, full of accusation. "And what makes you think this is a pirate crew?"

"Because the captain is a pirate. One who tried to kidnap me even."

She hesitated. "That isn't true."

"Yes, it is," said a voice from behind me—a deep voice, a strong voice, the voice of Chrysaor.

Joen took her dagger from my neck. She stared over my shoulder with fear in her eyes. I turned to face my onetime assailant.

The blue-skinned pirate smiled, the expression at once comfortable and out of place. "Though really, I wasn't after you, child. You are of no consequence." Chryasor said.

"Then you wanted the stone," I said.

"What stone—" Joen began.

I cut her off. "And you're still after the stone, aren't you?" I said. "That's the artifact you want this crew to help you recover. You know where to find it, don't you?"

"You are very perceptive," the blue man said. "But you shouldn't tip your hand so easily. Your one advantage is knowledge your opponent does not possess."

My mind was swirling. "Where is the stone?" I cried.

Chrysaor laughed, a bubbly laugh that reminded me, for some reason, of my childhood in the High Forest. "You don't even know what you had, child, and so you do not deserve it. And so you have lost it, and so you will never recover it." He jabbed my left shoulder and looked down at my leg. "And so you will die."

My hand again dropped to the hilt of my stiletto, but Chrysaor ignored me. He swung the inn's door open wide and stepped inside.

"So what do you think, friends?" he cried, raising his voice for the first time. Shall we set sail come springtime?" A great cheer went up within, followed by another.

"Joen, I have to tell you something," I whispered.

She looked at me—glared at me. "You should not have come," she said. She pushed past me into the inn, slamming the door behind her.

Chapter Fourteen

By the time I returned to *Sea Sprite*, the snow had turned to rain, and my whole body—along with the whole city—was soaked through and chilled to the bone.

Almost the entire crew was still hauling boxes and crates of cargo out of the hold. But no one was hauling anything belowdecks. I was somewhat surprised. We had been in port long enough that most of the stuff should have been offloaded. Most of the food and supplies should have been securely stowed within.

I reached the wharf just as Drizzt and his friends trudged down the docks.

"Ready to go?" he asked me.

"Uh, I . . . I'm not sure."

He cocked his head. "I wasn't aware you had much to pack," he said. "Catti-brie and the others are gathering our supplies, and we plan to be off before nightfall today. Best you make ready quickly."

I paced up the dock, my heartbeat thudding in my ears, my head tumbling through all I had just seen. Joen. Chrysaor. Chrysaor was hunting the stone. I thought of the seer in Memnon and his prophecy. "He seeks what you seek . . . A stranger to these lands, of skin and manner." I swallowed. Could it be?

I turned back to face Drizzt. "I'm not coming with you," I blurted out.

Drizzt stared at me. "Give us a moment," he said, addressing his companions.

"Of course," said Wulfgar. "We'll see to securing some horses." He walked past me, patting me on the head with his giant hand. Bruenor followed, muttering something about "durned fool kids." Then Catti-brie wrapped me in a hug before skipping off after them.

"So you've found a better course than Malchor Harpell?" Drizzt asked when the others had left.

"I think I've found someone who knows where

the stone is. And that's why you were taking me to Malchor, isn't it?"

Drizzt's brow furrowed. "Are you sure of your source?" he asked.

"No," I said, hanging my head. And then I spoke aloud the fear I had kept hidden for the past several tendays. "You have no way of knowing that Malchor has any insight into the stone and my troubles, do you?"

Drizzt shook his head. "But I do know that my friends and I are willing to protect you on the journey, if you join us. Are you certain you wish to stay here and take this risk?"

I shrugged. I could hardly admit my true motives even to myself right then. "It's a risk either way," I said.

"It is indeed," Drizzt said as he rested his hand on my shoulder. "My friend, I am saddened that you will not be joining us on the road. But I admire your bravery."

"So you think I should stay here?"

"I think you have wisdom enough to decide for yourself," Drizzt said. "And you did not approach me to ask my advice, did you? You approached me to say goodbye."

I nodded.

"Then goodbye, and safe travels, Maimun. I hope you find everything you are looking for." Drizzt offered me one last nod of assurance, then walked away.

With a heavy heart, I turned back to face *Sea Sprite*. The captain stood at the bottom of the gangplank, shaking hands with a man in blue wizard robes. I reached them just as their conversation apparently ended.

I recognized the wizard: it was Robillard, the same wizard who had pulled me from the harbor in Memnon.

"What are you doing here?" I blurted out before I realized I had spoken.

"I have been hired by the Lords of Waterdeep," he said. "To accompany a newly commissioned vessel to hunt pirates."

"But I thought you worked for the Memnon city guard."

"Waterdeep pays better," Robillard said.

"But . . . What vessel?" I asked.

"Well, Captain Deudermont's, obviously." He shook his head in what I hoped was mock annoyance.

"Enough," Captain Deudermont cut in. "What are you doing here, Maimun? Drizzt and his friends have just left." He gestured to the end of the dock. "You'll have to hurry to catch him."

"I'm . . . I'm sorry, sir," I stammered. "I'm not going with Drizzt." I took a deep breath, then relayed what I saw at the Shank. As I reached the end of my tale, my stomach filled with butterflies. "You once said that you and your crew would help me on my journey, sir. Can you help me go after Chrysaor?"

"Things have changed, Maimun. We are no longer a simple merchant crew," Deudermont said, his voice taking an air of formality. "We are now commissioned to hunt pirates. Dangerous work in the best of circumstances."

"Chrysaor is a pirate, sir," I said.

Robillard looked down at me. "I know of this Chrysaor. He's an underling pirate, not a captain. Serves—"

"Asbeel, I know," I cut in.

"Pinochet, actually, last I'd heard," Robillard said. "Who's Asbeel?"

"Oh, um, another pirate. I got confused." I wasn't quite sure why I was lying to Robillard, and based on his disapproving stare, Deudermont wasn't so sure either. But the captain did not say anything.

"Well, Chrysaor's a water genasi, not exactly common in the city," Robillard said.

"A what?" I asked. I had heard the term before, but could not place it.

"Genasi, descended of creatures of the elemental planes. He's got the blood of a water elemental in him."

"But . . . Aren't water elementals just, you know, water? How can they have kids?"

"Elemental creatures, not elementals specifically," Robillard said, rolling his eyes at my ignorance. "Maybe his great-great-great grandmother was a water nymph, and his great-great-great-grandfather was damned lucky," Robillard said, laughing at his own joke. When he saw we weren't joining in, he shrugged. "In any case, I can keep eyes on him easily enough."

I looked from Robillard to Deudermont, my eyes pleading. "If you help me, I'll do anything. I can fight. I can clean the bilge or the galley. Whatever you wish."

Deudermont sized me up. "You made good account of yourself on the last voyage. You have sharp eyes, and I could use a good lookout."

"So does that mean you will help me?" I asked.

Deudermont nodded. "Now grab some crates and follow the crew. We've a new ship to prepare."

I was off and running before the captain had finished giving his order. My goal seemed so much closer than it had even a day before. And, I dared to think, so was Joen.

CHAPTER FIFTEEN

The new ship, which Captain Deudermont named *Sea Sprite*—prompting among the crew a long series of jokes about his creativity—was beautiful, for sure. She was smaller than the old *Sea Sprite*, sleeker, with a different cut to the sails that would supposedly let her run faster and turn more sharply than any other ship on the seas. She was built to overtake a pirate ship in a chase, but not to overpower her.

But she was not built for the comfort of her crew. On the old ship, our quarters had been cramped. On the new vessel we were packed in so tightly it was a wonder no one was crushed to death while sleeping.

The galley was about half the size of our old one. Every time Tonnid or Lucky asked me to play cards, I turned them down. I didn't want to get stuck with any of their lousy shifts on the new ship.

In truth, we didn't have much time to spare for games. And none of us were given shore leave for more than a day at a time. Instead we spent our hours on deck, with a pair of swordmasters hired by the Lords of Waterdeep to train the crew.

For three months we sat in port, and for all three we drilled.

At first, Deudermont told me he wanted to keep me from fighting pirates once the ship set sail. He said I would be of more use in the crow's nest. But I finally wore him down with my constant begging, and he agreed it couldn't hurt for me to have some formal training in combat tactics and swordplay.

I was part of the crew, fully and completely. It should have made me happy. But the drills were more difficult than anything I'd tried to do before. My condition, while no longer worsening, left me terribly clumsy at best. The instructors were merciless, not accepting any excuses. The crew never passed an opportunity to laugh at my stumbles.

R.A. & GENO SALVATORE

Each night I would find a note from Robillard on my cot. He magically watched Chrysaor, who made no attempt to hide his actions. Like us, Chrysaor couldn't set sail until the winter storms had passed Waterdeep. But he did everything he could to prepare his crew to leave come spring. Shortly after the meeting in the tavern, Robillard left me a note that told me Chrysaor had purchased a ship, a two-master called *Lady Luck*. Later notes detailed the supplies Chrysaor bought each day. It was clear he and his crew were stocking the ship for a long, long journey. Each note ended the same way: "So when are you going to pay me for this service?" followed by Robillard's overly grandiose signature.

Then one day, six tendays yet before the vernal equinox, a burst of warm air flowed up from the south, and Waterdeep found herself thawing.

I came above deck, wrapped in my winter clothes, along with the whole crew. We had the day off, but the quarters below were so cramped that no one desired to stay put. We were to begin the next day with tactical training—which I guess meant moving as a unit—and we were all pleased, as we expected it to be less physically taxing than the sword fighting we had been learning.

But the air was warm, and the sun was bright, and we found ourselves distracted by a strange sight at that time of year: sails.

A single ship made her way through the still-icy waters of Waterdeep Harbor, headed for open seas. She was far from our berth, and the glare of the brilliant sun on the ice made her hard to distinguish. But somehow I knew exactly which ship she was.

I rushed to the captain's cabin and banged my fist against the door. "She's leaving! She's leaving! Captain!"

The door swung open, and I nearly tumbled in. Captain Deudermont stood before me, fully decked out in his regal captain's attire; behind him, Robillard appeared to be laughing. At me, I knew.

"Who is leaving?"

"Jo—uh, Chrysaor's ship. *Lady Luck*. She's leaving, right now, and we gotta go catch her."

Deudermont ushered me inside, motioning to a comfortable seat at the round oak table, between the wizard and Lucky, who had been appointed the boarding crew's tactical leader, a position of high honor. I gave my friend a brief smile as I took my seat, but if he noticed he paid me no heed.

"Robillard, what has your scrying revealed?" Deudermont asked, taking a seat across from me.

"Memory going in your old age, captain? I just told you."

"Yes, and now you will tell our newest arrival," Deudermont said, gesturing at me. "The short version will do fine."

Robillard rolled his eyes. "Captain Chrysaor and his ship have left port and are making slow speed to the south," he said.

"And beyond that?" Deudermont leaned comfortably back into his chair, seeming almost disinterested.

"There's a great storm brewing to the north," The wizard replied. "If it turns south, it'll put Waterdeep under several feet of snow in three days' time."

"Now Maimun," said Deudermont. "What do you suppose would happen to a ship caught in such a storm?"

"She'd be covered in snow," I said. "I don't care."

"You should care," Deudermont snarled. I had never seen him angry like that. "The crew care for you; you should care about them."

"I do, but—" I started, but the captain cut me off.

"But, you care more about yourself and your own goals."

"You promised, sir. You promised you would help me however you can."

"I did. But this I cannot do."

"Why not? They have the guts to sail out, why don't you?"

"It's not about guts. They risk utter disaster, for small gain. I will not take that risk."

"Small gain? My life is small gain?" I realized my mistake as soon as the words left my mouth.

"Your life is at greater risk if we sail out than if we stay here. And your life is not more important than the lives of all the rest of the crew."

I had heard that speech before, but from the other side. My life was more important than the whole crew of a ship, Perrault had said. But he had also said, protect first the ones you love.

"Captain, we're supposed to be pirate hunters, right?" I asked, putting on my most naïve expression. "Well, there's a pirate ship. And she's sailing away. Why aren't we hunting her?"

Lucky turned to look at me then at Deudermont, his eyes wide.

Deudermont rose up. "This conversation is over. You are all dismissed."

I started to say something, but Deudermont had already turned his back on me. Lucky punched my shoulder lightly, then headed for the door. Robillard, still sitting next to me, barely contained a laugh; and not for my sake, I knew. If Captain Deudermont hadn't been there, Robillard would have been taunting me mercilessly.

With my shoulders slumped, I wandered back out onto the deck. The rest of the crew was enjoying the warm weather, but I felt cold inside, and no amount of sun would change that. I slunk below, fell into my bunk, and drifted off to a fitful sleep, and dreamed I had followed Drizzt and his friends out of Waterdeep.

CHAPTER SIXTEEN

I awoke to a grating, grinding sound and a vibration in the ship. The waves swelled up beneath us, moving us far more than any ship should when tied safely to a dock. Either the storm had arrived early and the seas were tossing beneath us, or . . .

I leaped from my cot and raced to the ladder, barefoot and bare-chested, wearing only the breeches I'd slept in. Up I went, into the afternoon sun, just in time to catch the spray as *Sea Sprite* cut through a wave.

I glanced around, hardly believing what I was seeing. Captain Deudermont had the helm, and the sails were set and full of the wind blowing down from the north. The crew moved about in a slow waltz, securing a line here, untying one there, following the captain's orders almost before he called them.

"Mister Maimun, to the helm," the captain called. "After you dress yourself, that is." Without a word—I couldn't have found one if I'd tried—I dropped down the ladder and raced to my cot, quickly gathered my things, and sprinted back to the deck. The sway of the ship on open water beneath my feet felt wonderful.

"Yes, sir," I said as I skidded to a halt before the captain, trying to sound formal and calm.

"Relieve Mister McCanty in the crow's nest, if you please," Deudermont said.

"Yes, sir. And thank you, sir."

"Don't thank me," he said tersely. "Thank your friend Lucky. He polled the crew, and they agreed, to a man, to take the incredible risk and pursue our blue friend."

I could barely draw breath as I walked to the crow's nest.

My head was still spinning when I reached the top of the mainmast. The mast was shorter than on the old *Sea Sprite*, so the view was not as good and the bucket was smaller—or I had grown. But the ship moved with a speed unlike anything the previous one could have managed, and the chill wind in my face was refreshing indeed.

I took it all in: the smell of the air and the feel of the wind; the view of the crew moving about, a perfectly choreographed dance; the shining sun reflected off the sea, and off the—

"Iceberg! Ahead, off the port bow!" I yelled.

We cut sharply, avoiding the massive chunk of floating ice. And the next, and the next, and on and on, huge bergs drifting down from the Sea of Moving Ice. The thaw had dislodged them from their winter rest, but it was not warm enough to melt them. It would be a dangerous journey indeed. I hoped it would be worth it.

My mind wandered back to the previous summer. I had seen only snippets of actual combat on that journey, had watched much of it from a porthole in the hold of the ship, until a particularly nasty troll pirate had climbed aboard. I had defended the ship from the troll and had eventually knocked the foul thing from the boat.

After the fight, Captain Deudermont had offered me a place on his crew, citing my courage. But it had not been courage, it had been self-preservation that drove me. The troll had found me, and would have killed me had I not fought back. I looked down at my scar. That was the end result of my so-called courage.

And I was leading the crew into trouble yet again. We were following a pirate ship—all because of me, because the crew had agreed to help me. I remembered Tasso, a sailor aboard *Sea Sprite* during the other fight. He had been wounded, and had died in the bed next to mine. More could die because of me and my selfishness, I knew. Would Lucky fall, or Tonnid, or even Captain Deudermont?

I shook the thought from my head. This time would be different, I vowed. We would capture Chrysaor and force him to tell us where the stone was. And if anyone died in the trying, it would be me.

"Look alive, Maimun!" I caught sight of Lucky down below hefting a coil of rope over his shoulder. He looked up at me, his eyes shaded from the sun. "Why the long face? Ye're going to get yer pirate after all!"

"Seems so!" I called out. "I can't thank you enough!"

"How's about you join me and Tonnid in a game of cards later on then, eh? We got a few chores we wouldn't mind putting on the table for a lucky fellar like yerself." Lucky's face broke out into a wide grin.

I nodded and laughed along with him. And that was all the confirmation I needed that we were on the right path after all.

For seven long days we followed *Lady Luck*, each colder than the last. The ship had turned due west, then northwest, and was heading out into open water far, far from shore. We never caught sight of her, but Robillard kept his magical eyes upon her.

He also kept his eyes on the northern storm, which hit Waterdeep right on schedule, bringing nearly three feet of snow. Even if we had wanted to turn back, we couldn't. The harbor was sealed shut.

I remembered the voyage from Baldur's Gate to Waterdeep: the constant tacking, the long nights in fear of a berg, the cold so deep it felt as if I'd never feel warmth again.

Each day, I took my post in the crow's nest. The biting wind was brutal. I wrapped Perrault's cloak around me, but it wasn't the magic that kept me warm. I leaned into that frigid wind. I thought of what might lie at the end of the journey, and the cold never touched me.

On the seventh day out from Waterdeep, I sighted a dark line of clouds, due west and moving toward us.

"Storm! Dark clouds ahead, due west!" I called down.

Everyone abovedecks halted whatever they were doing. Then a moment later, they began again, working more furiously than ever.

"Hold course," Deudermont called out.

Right into the storm, I thought. The man who had initially refused to sail out of port for fear of a winter storm, was ordering us to hold course directly into one.

"What do you see, Maimun?" Deudermont yelled.

"No bergs ahead, just the storm, sir," I called. How had Robillard not scryed it? Or perhaps he had, but he and the captain had kept it secret from the d thirteen, I knew; her birthday was in

Luck drew closer, our catapult sent another
urning pitch into the sky. I watched its arc,
ed on the black clouds of the approaching
eemed to drift on the air, in defiance of
ving oh so slowly toward its target.
slowly, toward *Lady Luck*'s mainmast.
d *Lady Luck*'s crow's nest.
es widened in terror. Joen ducked down
ow's nest.
laming bucket skipped off the mast barely
above her, sending the thing swaying. But
ic did not break, and the whole bucket
d through the furled rigging into the
w. Joen poked her head up again, her head
p and down. Sobbing?
laughing. Thirteen and fearless. That was

nned *Lady Luck*'s deck. She had no catapult,
med to me that we would get many more
ore the ships closed the last few hundred
t a pirate stood on the forward deck, waving
in tiny circles, chanting. An odd time to be

crew? The captain would have no reason to conceal something like that, would he?

"Just the storm? Are you sure?" I got the distinct feeling he knew something I did not.

I peered out into the distance scanning the horizon in all directions. Nothing north, nothing south, nothing east, a storm west . . .

A storm, with a white spot on it. A growing white spot. Sails.

"Sail ho! Due west, and it looks like she's closing!"

"Very good," the captain called. "Can you make her heading?"

"Looks like she's sailing right at us, sir."

"Very good. Mister Lucky?"

"Oh, right," Lucky, who was standing beside the captain, said. "All hands make ready for battle!"

As *Lad*

bucket of b

a trail of r

storm. It

gravity, m

Oh so

Towar

My e

into the cr

The f

four feet

the ceran

plummete

water belc

bobbing

No,

Joen.

I sca

and it se

shots bef

yards. Bu

his arms

CHAPTE

Whoosh!

The catapult on

throwing a ceramic buc

the air, spinning end

water three hundred yar

A ranging shot. Anc

I looked across the v

ship, to the bustle of act

spot of yellow in the cr

Joen sat there with he

piercing green eyes, anc

age. And I knew she loo

singing and dancing, I thought.

Crack! I whipped back to look at our foredeck. A massive fireball burst directly over our own catapult. The whole catapult crew dropped to the deck. Small fires sprang up all around them, and fingers of flame reached out for the stacked buckets of pitch.

The crew rose up and immediately began to scramble, pails of water in hand. I tried not to imagine what would happen if the fire reached the pile of pitch before they could extinguish it. The blaze of fire, the screams of pain, the smell of burning flesh . . .

"They've got a wizard!" I called down. "Forward deck, wearing pirate clothes." A bolt of lightning arced out from the hands of the wizard. "He's casting a sp—"

The lighting struck the side of the crow's nest, splintered right through the wood, and crashed into me. Energy jolted through my chest, and I flew up into the air.

I squeezed my eyes shut and held my breath, waiting to plummet onto the deck below.

But a second later, I realized, I was not falling.

I opened my eyes.

I was drifting, as light as a feather. I looked at my hand and caught a glimpse of the gold band circling my finger. I remembered gliding down from the wall in Baldur's Gate, Perrault's hand in my own. He had given me the magical ring then, but I had completely forgotten I still wore it.

The deck drifted up to meet me, slowly, dreamlike.

From below, I heard several crewmen gasp. At first I thought they were merely astonished by my gentle fall. Then I looked down.

The ship was sailing out from under me. I would not land on the deck, but in the frigid ocean beyond!

I snatched my stiletto from my belt. I thrust it into the sail, or what little of the canvas was exposed. My fine dagger cut through the sail as if it were paper. I heard a few lines snap. But my momentum slowed.

At last I came to a stop, dangling ten feet above the deck.

The wind picked up. The crew scrambled around the deck below me.

"Help!" I called out weakly. But my words were lost in the growing storm.

A fine white powder of snow churned all around me. I peered through the tear in the sail at *Lady Luck*'s forward deck, my heart in my throat. The wizard who had attacked me had disappeared. But her captain, Chrysaor, still held fast to the wheel. Snow settled on the crossbeams of her rigging, on her rails, on Chrysaor's violet hat. Then, without warning or any apparent reason, Chrysaor flung his hands from the wheel and stepped back. I took in a sharp breath. He mounted the forward deck railing. For a moment he stood there, riding the storm, his blue-skinned face lifted into the wind, his ocean white hair whipping out behind him. He turned to flash me a wicked grin. And then, he plunged into the sea.

"No!" I called out. "Captain! Chrysaor is abandoning his ship!" I looked down at our own deck just as Captain Deudermont's hat blew off, lost to the storm.

The sky grew dark. The sail I clung to whipped around, as if it were trying to buffet me loose. My arm ached. I could not hold on much longer. No one was coming to help me.

I pulled my dagger free, kicking off from the sail.

I landed hard, sending numbing pain coursing up my left leg.

As soon as I hit the deck, the storm unleashed its full fury. The air was thick with snow, and sleet blew sidelong across the deck. The wind swirled. Those few sails that were open threatened to tear from their rigging. But they could not catch and harness the wind, and we did not move. The other ship was completely obscured. The crew slipped and slid, and I slid with them, finding my balance impossible to keep on the slick deck in the tossing seas.

Only Captain Deudermont held his ground, his grip firm on the wheel.

At last I pulled myself up to the railing and glanced down at the rolling ocean. But I could see nothing but white-capped waves. Chrysaor was gone, racing to safety beneath the sea.

Suddenly the deck beneath my feet heaved. The whole ship rose into the air, caught on a huge swell. The water carried us with it, carried us faster than the wind ever had.

A voice cried out over the wind—Lucky's voice. "Captain! She's—" The rest of his warning was garbled in the wind.

But his meaning became clear a second later, as *Lady Luck* came racing up alongside *Sea Sprite*, her deck barely ten feet from ours.

With a colossal bang, her mainmast and ours collided.

Both ships stopped in their tracks.

I, however, did not. Nor did the rest of the crew.

We flew across the deck. I crashed into a rolling barrel and bumped into Lucky before I finally came to rest at the forward deck.

The snow cleared just long enough to reveal Captain Deudermont, standing firm and tall at the helm, holding his sword high. The wind died just enough to hear his voice calling out to us.

"To arms," he cried, "and to the rail! To the fight!"

"To arms!" echoed Lucky, scrambling to his feet.

CHAPTER EIGHTEEN

I watched as the men of *Sea Sprite* rose up unsteadily around me. They shook off their bumps and bruises. They drew their weapons.

Then they raced to the pirate ship's rail.

We had trained hard the last few months, in swordplay and in tactics. But in the span of that last second before the throng of pirates crashed into the crew, all that training disappeared.

The fight descended into chaos.

I huddled behind an overturned barrel. I had promised the captain that I would stay out of the fighting. And I meant to hold fast to that vow. After all, with my leg aching and my still clumsy swordwork, what good could I possibly do?

Sounds of steel on steel echoed across the water, with battle cries turning fast to howls of pain.

The first time a cry of pain ripped through the air, I found my breath hard to come by. I watched as the battle lines formed and broke, as the throng surged toward the rail, then halted and pushed back the other way. I watched as the snow piled up on the deck, listened as the wood of the tangled ships creaked and groaned against the strain, against the wind.

I watched in horror as the snow piles turned red.

I peered around the barrel to see a man go tumbling over the rail, screaming all the way into the icy water. I could not tell if it was one of ours or one of theirs.

I wedged myself farther behind the barrel and hugged my knees. I had brought all of it about, I reminded myself. I had started the voyage. But here I was, hiding, while men died for me. I could hold back no longer.

Gathering all my courage, I pushed back the barrel and stood up. I took a step, then another, then broke into a run across the slick deck. I would leap the rail, join the fray. I flicked my dagger into a long blade.

And then I saw her.

Around the side of the melee, a tiny figure moved: a girl with hair the color of wheat and the purest green eyes. She held a dagger in each hand, and walked like a warrior, stepping lightly and in perfect balance.

And then she saw me.

Twenty yards separated us, but I felt as if we were standing face to face. Her expression was as cold as the storm, her teeth gritted, and her jaw set.

Joen crossed the deck at a run, leaping the rail in a single, graceful leap, landing but a few yards in front of me. The wind picked up again, drowning out the sounds of combat. The snow came down faster, obscuring the battle still raging around us.

I held up my arms, sword out wide, trying to indicate that I meant no harm. Joen rushed toward me, her arms tight to her body. For a moment I thought she was going to embrace me.

Instead, she punched out with the pommel of the dagger. It slammed me in the forehead and sent me reeling. I fell and skidded halfway across the deck.

I lifted my sword and looked up, expecting her to be right atop me. I rose unsteadily to my feet, my weapon at the ready.

"Never drop your guard in a fight, eh?" she said, stalking toward me. "That's a free lesson for you. The next one's gonna cost you, got it?"

I brought my sword up, touching the blade to my forehead right where her blow had landed, then snapping it back down in mock salute. "So you have more lessons for me, then?" I quipped, settling into the stance the Waterdeep swordmasters had taught me.

"Many more, kid," she promised, spitting the last word like an insult.

I knew she was angry at me so I decided to allow her the first attacks until her rage played itself out.

Left, right, left, she slashed with her daggers, aiming not for me but for my blade. She meant to knock my sword out of line—her eight-inch daggers would not reach me if she could not move her body past my sword.

With a simple twist of my wrist, I kept my sword in line with her through each contact. The numbness in my left side was almost a memory. The quality of my swordplay surprised even me.

"Feeling better yet?" I asked sarcastically.

"You're still standing."

"So that's a yes?"

She snarled and repeated her attack. If she meant to kill me, she surely could have in that initial strike. But neither was she dropping her weapons or her guard. My pulse quickened. Perhaps she did mean to kill me after all.

Left, right, left; but that time, as the second left hit my blade, she took a quick step to her left and brought her right-hand dagger close to her chest. As I twisted the blade in, trying to keep her at bay, she stepped toward me. I had not reacted quickly enough to her step, and the angle was wrong. When I tried to compensate, to angle my sword farther in toward her, I merely hit her right-hand dagger.

She shuffled toward me, quickstepping in and disengaging her left dagger at the same time. I tried to pull my sword in, to cut off her line of attack, but she pushed with her right dagger, and I could not maneuver my much longer sword into a good position.

She thrust out with her left hand, blade tip leading, and all I could do was fall back to my left and skip away. I felt the rush of air as the dagger swept past my head, felt the tiny prick of pain, felt the little drop of warm liquid dripping from the nick on my ear.

I hopped back a few steps, settling again into my defensive pose; again, she did not press.

"I suppose I'm feeling a bit better now," she said. Her eyes were still icy cold as she crept forward, her daggers at the ready.

"You're about to feel a lot worse," I said.

I would not let her lead again. As she approached, I thrust out, once, twice, and again, short jabs that did not come close to hitting the mark. But neither did she get close enough to attack me.

But I could keep her at bay for only so long like that. My sword was light, but still heavier than her daggers. I was expending more energy than she, and I would surely tire faster.

She knew it too, and she allowed me my simple attack routines.

I jabbed again, a short stab from my elbow, my body staying still and in balance. Joen shifted her weight, staying out of my reach, her daggers at the ready but a parry not necessary. I started to repeat the motion, but planned to push off with my back leg, drop my trailing arm, and fully extend my sword arm. I would reach out fully three feet farther than the short jab, and the whole move would take only a fraction of a second longer. I would catch her completely off guard.

But I hesitated. Could I really hurt her? Could I really kill Joen?

My body reacted when my mind could not, and I did indeed attack, but there was little strength behind my lunge. And Joen was not surprised by the move at all, anyway. She dropped into a crouch, bringing both daggers up in a cross, catching the bottom of my blade and driving it up.

Before I could retract, she pushed off with her legs from her deep crouch directly at me. She kept her right hand up, her dagger holding my sword at bay; her left she thrust forward, tip leading, right for my chest.

I brought my trailing left arm around in desperation, and only through some luck did I manage to contact her thrusting arm and drive it aside.

But she still had a vastly superior position to mine. She brought her right hand in, and though I found my sword free, once again she was far too close for me to use it effectively.

Instead, I bulled ahead before she could line up her strikes. I shoved my left forearm into her chest and pushed off with all my might.

She brought both her daggers in from the sides. I felt them hit me, but she was falling backwards and there was no strength in the swings. They did not even cut through my tunic.

She let herself fall, rolling backwards with perfect grace, then coming to her feet and skipping back another step, out of my reach once more.

I took a breath. "You fight well," I said.

"That makes one of us."

"For a girl," I finished.

"Still just one of us."

I growled and took a step forward, ready to strike, but stopped short. "Why are you doing this?" I asked. "Are you really trying to kill me?"

She opened her mouth as if to speak, then closed it, shaking her head.

"Answer—" Before I could finish, she rushed forward again. She swung her arms as one, both blades moving at the same time, in the same direction, barely an inch apart. As she swung her swords, she moved her body the opposite direction. If she hit my blade, she would drive it away from herself, and she would be upon me in an instant.

I stepped back furiously, trying to keep her

weaving dance in front of me, trying to keep my sword between us.

I managed five steps, then my rear foot hit something solid.

The rail. I had run out of room. I had no retreat; and I did not know how to defend her attack.

So I didn't try. I swept my sword out, horizontal at eye level, the fine saber edge leading. Joen ducked, bringing her blades up to deflect and ensnare my sword.

But the slash was only a feint. The real attack was my body. I pushed off from the rail with all my might, colliding with her and driving her backward. I kept my legs pumping, kept pushing, preventing her from bringing her daggers to bear.

I pressed her straight back, across the deck, into the base of the mainmast. We crashed into the solid wood hard. I felt her breath leave her body. The daggers fell from her limp hands.

I stumbled back a step, dazed. Joen stayed with me, wrapping her arms around me for balance.

She buried her head in my shoulder, coughing and crying. I could not tell if the tears were from physical pain or some emotion.

I did not ask.

All I could do was let my own sword fall from my hand, and wrap my arms around her, holding her tight.

"I'm sorry," she whispered. "I was going to . . . I wanted to . . . I'm sorry."

"It's all right," I said. "I forgive you."

CHAPTER NINETEEN

The blizzard grew worse. The wind swirled and caught the sails of the two ships, twisting them one way or the other. Their fouled riggings groaned in protest.

Waves pulled the ships apart then slammed them back together again and again, deck to deck, with a great jarring impact and a crash that resounded like thunder.

Most of the crew of both ships were aboard *Lady Luck*. The pirate crew—outnumbered, captainless, facing a better armed and better trained crew—had surrendered, but the crew of *Sea Sprite* did not dare cross back to their own ship in that weather. Nor did anyone dare climb the masts to untangle the lines. Aboard *Lady Luck*, all of the men of both crews vanished belowdecks, evidently intending to ride out the storm in warmer quarters. Aboard *Sea Sprite*, two remained above.

Joen had settled in next to me. The pair of us rested against the mainmast, Perrault's magical cloak wrapped around us. While I wore it, the cloak never seemed especially large; it did not billow nor drag on the ground. But covering myself and Joen it seemed more a blanket than a cloak, and it wrapped around us both completely, a warm cocoon against the wind and the blowing snow.

Our ship looked terrible. The rail was broken in many places. Scorch marks scarred the deck near the catapult and on the mainmast. And our rigging was hopelessly tangled with that of the ship across the narrow stretch of water. But *Lady Luck* looked even worse. She listed steeply toward our portside as wave after wave rolled beneath her.

Joen's breathing had steadied, then slowed. At first it had frightened me, but when she nestled her head into my shoulder and snored loudly, I realized she had simply drifted off to sleep. I would have gladly followed her, but I told myself that if we both slept, I would lose my grip on the hem of the cloak, and the cloak would fall wide open to the furious elements. So I stayed awake, one hand holding the cloak closed, the other gripping, through the cloak's fabric, a rope tied around the mast. Joen could have her rest, I decided. I would protect her while she slept.

Besides, I had no idea where I would put my hands if I did not have something useful to do with them. I flushed red and shifted uncomfortably.

Joen stirred and looked up at me. Even in the fading light her eyes shone, emeralds boring into me. She could see what I was thinking, I knew it. She was about to toss off the cloak and storm off the deck.

But she did not. She merely gave me a curious smile, and wrapped her arms around my waist. Her arms were thin but strong, and her grip was tight as she pulled herself closer. She felt warm beside me, and I was grateful for it. I let go of the rope on the mast and put my arm around her shoulders, my hand resting awkwardly against her side. She did not seem to mind. She put her head down again on my shoulder, and a few moments later she was fast asleep.

I know not how long I stayed awake. Even as I dozed my dreams were filled with images of the here and now. The storm blew snow across the deck, falling in piles only to be shaken off again. The wind howled, and wood crashed against wood. And screams—real or imagined—echoed across the waves. Joen slept on my shoulder, her arms wrapped around me.

When I woke in the morning, it took me a good while to realize that I was indeed awake, and that the pair of polished black boots on the deck in front of me were indeed real.

"Look alive, sailors," Captain Deudermont said.

Joen and I both started. She jumped to her feet. But my cloak caught my ankles as I rose, and I tumbled back to the deck.

At that precise moment, the ship gave a mighty lurch. I skidded toward the broken rail on our starboard side, nearest *Lady Luck*. I could see a great hole in her hull just at the water line. I thought I saw a flicker of movement beyond the hole, but could not discern what it was before another wave rolled up against her, covering the hole. *Sea Sprite* gave another lurch beneath me. I grasped at the planks of the deck to prevent myself from sliding yet farther.

One man stood on *Lady Luck*'s rail—quite literally. Robillard rode the rail itself, seeming unfazed by the ship's sharp motion. He simply went about his business, waving his hands in some arcane gesture, mumbling some chant, and tossing what looked like blue ropes toward *Sea Sprite*.

The ropes stretched above the water and grabbed *Sea Sprite*'s rail. Some tied themselves there. Some grabbed the already-set lines and tied across. A net of sorts formed before my eyes.

Behind me, Captain Deudermont tapped his foot. I allowed myself to skid all the way to the rail. There I leaned against it to stand, and walked unsteadily across the deck.

I took my place beside Joen, who stood at attention in front of the man who was not her captain.

"You'll need better balance than that, Maimun, if you want to be a sailor," Captain Deudermont said.

"Yes, sir. Sorry, sir," I mumbled.

"As soon as Robillard has finished his work, you're going up the mast. We need to get untangled."

I swallowed. "Yes, sir. But why now?" Though the storm had given up much of its rage in the night, the winds still swirled around us. The last thing I wanted to do was to climb back up the mast. I pointed to the dark clouds above us. "Why not wait for the storm to blow out?"

Joen gave me a startled look, but only for a second; clearly, she did not think it wise to question the captain's orders.

I thought I caught a little smile flash over Deudermont's face. But when he spoke, he looked directly at Joen.

"*Lady Luck* is sinking," he said. Joen did not flinch. "We need to untangle, or she'll take us down with her."

"Yes, sir," I said for the third time.

"And you," he said, addressing Joen. "Did I not see you in the crow's nest aboard the other ship?"

"The gull's nest, aye, sir. That's my post, eh?"

I felt a strange elation climbing in my chest. Deudermont was sending Joen up the mast with me! My fear vanished. I knew there would be a lot of tough work. I knew there would be the ever-present danger of a fall, a danger made more keen by the blowing wind and the swaying of the ships. But working near Joen was worth any danger.

"Well then," the captain said to me, "you have another job before you climb the mast."

I hesitated a second, sorting out Deudermont's words. "I do, sir?" I asked.

"Yes. First you'll escort this young woman to our brig."

"But, sir, she's not a pirate," I said.

"And you'll not question your orders. Now get to it." With that, the captain turned and walked away.

Beside me, Joen chuckled. "Don't look so stunned, eh? Soon as he recognized me, I knew I'd be going below. Be a fool to think anything else."

"Well, I'm a fool then," I muttered.

She just laughed. "Oi, course you're a fool. Probably thought he'd be sending me up into the rigging with you, didn't you? Don't be a disobedient fool, though, he won't much like that, will he?" She started to walk to the hatch that led down to the hold, still chuckling.

I followed a few paces behind her.

"Oi, ain't you supposed to be escorting me to the brig?" she asked, looking over her shoulder at me.

"Ain't that what I'm doing, eh?" I replied, doing my best to imitate her accent. I was so happy to have her here, safe aboard *Sea Sprite*, that I couldn't help but joke a little.

"Then why am I walking in front?"

"Prisoners always walk in front," I quipped.

"Oh, yeah, right, so they can't stab the guard in the back, eh? You figure I'm gonna try and stab you?" She laughed, but her laugh turned into a painful cough. She stopped walking and doubled over, clutching at her chest.

"I think you already tried to stab me," I said. "And you got that cough instead."

Joen glared up at me, her eyes burning behind the veil of her hair. "That ain't funny," she said, her voice stern.

"It wasn't so funny when you cut my ear, either." I said, matching her tone.

Slowly she straightened, standing tall and proud, not looking away. The intensity of her stare was intimidating, and it was all I could do to maintain eye contact. But I would not look away.

"Prisoners walk in front," I growled, motioning toward the hatch.

She did not say another word all the way to the brig.

CHAPTER TWENTY

Half a dozen of us took to the masts a short while later. Three *Sea Sprite* sailors accustomed to working in the rigging climbed up from each deck. There was almost no activity beneath us. Only Robillard stood on deck, or rather sat, looking quite comfortable on the sterncastle of *Lady Luck*, his feet dangling over the rail. His magical net stretched between the two ships. It looked solid despite the fact that it was formed of what appeared to be tendrils of blue light. As the ships pulled apart, the net stretched, but the gaps did not seem to grow. As the ships crashed together once again, the net swelled upward, as if a breeze from below had caught a bit of fabric and made it billow. There was no way for someone to fall through, I hoped.

Soon after we had reached the fouled riggings, it seemed the gods decided we should not be allowed to escape our fates.

The wind blew steadily and with such force that it was all I could do to maintain a grip on the ropes. Up here, so high above the deck, the air was much colder, and with the wind whipping about there was no way I could keep Perrault's cloak wrapped around me. I felt the stinging burn of the cold and the numbness of frostbite creeping into my fingertips. It was a welcome relief from the other numbness, which had nearly disappeared.

I did not complain. Instead I let my anger warm me. At first it was simply a vague sense of anger, a hatred of the way things had been for as long as I could remember. But then my anger found focus. First at Asbeel, who had stolen so much from me; then at Chrysaor, the blue-skinned pirate captain, who had led me so far astray only to disappear. Then at Deudermont, my captain, who had locked up Joen when he should have been sending her up here to work with me.

And there my anger found a home: Joen.

She had attacked me, had cut my ear. It still stung quite a bit, especially in the cold. Then she had called me a fool, and refused my orders. And that was just since sunrise!

I lay my torso down on a thin crossbeam. My feet braced against the mast, and my arms reached out for a tangle of rigging. As *Lady Luck* was sinking anyway, our orders were not so much to untangle the ships, as to free *Sea Sprite* from the burden of the crippled vessel. At each point of entanglement, I would seek the lines that belonged to the pirate vessel and cut them loose, then move on to the next point I could reach.

The whole journey had been for Joen, I realized. I had told myself I was seeking the stone, but it was a lie. I had never really believed we'd get any information from Chrysaor. I should have gone with Drizzt to see Malchor Harpell. He would have pointed me in the right direction.

My hand snaked down a line of rigging from *Lady Luck*.

But instead I had followed Joen out to sea, to save her from the pirate crew she had willingly joined. And after I had saved her, all she could do was laugh at me and call me a fool.

I sliced through the rigging with such force, I nearly sent my dagger down with the falling rope. Again, I located a line, and again I tore through it. At each line I found a new reason to vent my rage.

I was still lying on the thin wooden crossbeams, when I felt something graze the back of my head. It felt like someone wearing a heavy cloak had walked past me, and the cloak had brushed against me. My heart beat a little faster.

I tried to turn, but I couldn't twist around from my already-precarious position without risking a fall. So instead I had to pull myself back to the mast, then straighten up. In the time it took me to reestablish myself, whatever had hit me had disappeared.

It must have been a loose line, I forced myself to think. Again I moved out along the beam, making sure my position was more secure, and I could turn around if needed. Sure enough, after a minute I felt something. It was not so much contact as something rushing past my head.

I turned quickly, but saw nothing.

I squinted. A tiny black shape spiraled in the distance. But it remained indistinct, blurred by the blowing snow, its dark shape uncertain against the equally dark midday sky. It was too small to be Asbeel. I let out a breath I didn't know I had been holding.

I watched the shape move, graceful and smooth. It seemed equally at home riding a gust of wind or cutting right through one. The air suddenly cleared, the storm giving us a reprieve, and the speck flew back to the mast.

I gasped and very nearly lost my perch. A raven!

I knew it could be no ordinary raven, for no ordinary bird would brave the weather, and a raven would never be so far out at sea.

The bird alighted on the crossbeam in front of me and stared into my eyes. It was the same bird I had seen in Memnon. What on Toril was it doing here?

Its chest puffed out proudly, the bird opened its beak.

And it cawed. It raised its head and gave a slight nod—a truly odd thing to see a bird do. Then it took off, its wings beating hard, cutting through the snow to the southeast.

The raven disappeared from sight for a minute, then circled back in, landing again in the same spot. It let out a caw and took off again, repeating the circle.

I peered off after it, trying to track its flight, trying

to see what the bird so obviously wanted to show me. But I saw nothing but swirling sleet and darkness.

Darkness . . .

"Land ahead!" I screamed as loudly as I could. But my words were lost in the storm. I waved my arms, trying to signal the captain, or Robillard, or anyone below, but I was invisible in the blizzard.

I scurried to the mast, shimmying along the rigging. I had to climb down and warn Deudermont.

But I was not fast enough.

With a tremendous crash, *Sea Sprite* slammed into the beach.

I grasped with frozen hands for a rope, a beam, anything. The grinding noise of wood splintering on rock echoed even above the wind. My hands tangled in a pair of lines, and I regained my balance. I withdrew my hand to find blood on my forearm. The rope had cut me, but thankfully it was not deep.

Then *Lady Luck* hit us. The jarring impact sent me spinning over the rigging and down toward the choppy sea.

But as before, I drifted downward—like a feather on a light breeze. I wafted clear of the wreckage, until I landed with a roll on the beach.

The sand was soaked, but no snow had accumulated. Numerous jagged rocks lined the shore. *Sea Sprite* had run aground against several of the rocks, I saw, but she had mostly hit sand and plowed forward. Half her hull was beyond the water line.

Lady Luck had not been so fortunate. As far as I could tell, she had crashed against *Sea Sprite*, then bounced off some rocks. The waves were pulling her back out to sea, dragging *Sea Sprite* along with her, where they would both surely sink.

I stumbled to my feet, dizzy but unhurt, just as the exodus began. Men on *Sea Sprite* threw down lines and climbed onto the beach. Those on *Lady Luck* simply jumped into the icy water and swam.

Lady Luck's hull breach had grown, and apparently had torn open the brig, for the pirate crew were among those swimming most desperately—battling waves and narrowly avoiding the rocks.

I saw Lucky and Captain Deudermont walking down the beach. I breathed a sigh of relief. Tonnid was climbing down a line from *Sea Sprite*.

But there was one person missing. Apparently *Sea Sprite*'s jail had not broken, and no one had thought to open it.

I ran to the ship. *Sea Sprite* listed badly to port as she slid backward into the open sea. Tonnid was just dropping off the line as I started to climb up. He mumbled something at me as I approached. But I did not reply. I simply clambered right past him and pulled myself up onto the deck.

The mainmast was leaning dangerously, ripping up planks from the deck. It looked as if it could fall into the water at any moment. The deck was slick with sleet. I ran as fast as I could manage, slipping often but always bouncing right back up to my feet.

I reached the hatch that led below and threw it open. I raced down the ladder, through the hold, fighting against the ship's list, feeling the slide, knowing I was nearly out of time.

Joen sat patiently, calmly, on the brig floor. Her legs were crossed, her head rested on her hand, her elbow on her knee. She was the only person in the brig.

"You came back for me," she said quietly when I skidded to a halt at the iron-barred door of the cell. She made no attempt to rise though.

"Of course I did."

She offered the slightest smile and rose slowly to her feet. "Took you long enough, eh?"

"Well, you know, it's kind of a long walk from the beach," I said, scanning the wall where the cell keys would normally hang. The pegs were all empty. "We ran aground, didn't you notice?"

"Not much of a view from here," she said. "So you got off the ship, then got back on? Not very efficient, are you?"

"I got thrown off the ship, actually," I said. I dropped to my knees and scrabbled around on the ground, looking for where the keys might have rolled.

"What, your captain kicked you off? Oi, what did you do to him, then?" she said laughing, and she leaned against the bars. I could feel her watching my increasingly desperate movements.

"No, I mean, literally thrown off the ship. When we ran aground." There was no sign of the keys. A few crates were piled against the port wall; by their haphazard arrangement I could see that they had fallen there in the crash.

"So how're you alive, then? Seems that'd be a long way to fall."

"There's a lot about me you don't know," I said. "I have powers you can't even fathom."

She laughed. "More likely you landed in the mud,

eh? I bet you sank in good and deep, and they had to pull you out by the hair!"

"Then I'd be covered in mud, wouldn't I?" I snapped, and she fell silent. I reached behind the crates, hoping the keys had tumbled there—and I found open air and cold, blowing wind. I pulled back, startled.

"Something wrong?" Joen asked. For the first time there was a note of trepidation in her voice.

I couldn't answer. I just pushed against the crates, shoving them roughly out of the way and revealing a small but not insignificant hole in the wall, leading directly out into the storm.

I turned back to Joen. Her face was ashen, her eyes wide. Without a word, she sat back down, put one elbow on one knee and dropped her head onto her hand.

The ship continued to list, but I hardly felt it. I lost my balance and slipped to the floor, but I made no effort to right myself. My mind whirled, searching for an answer, for a way to open the cell without the key. But the brig was built solidly, and there was no way we could pry open the door. I didn't know how to pick a lock, and I did not have the necessary tools anyway.

The keys had fallen through the hole in the wall, I was sure of it. But there was no similar hole on the other side, within the prison, through which Joen could escape.

I looked back at Joen. I wanted to say something, but the words sounded hollow in my head before they ever reached my mouth.

With a jerk, *Sea Sprite* slid further backward, and I could feel the deck beneath my feet heaving in the high surf. Soon we would be out on the open sea. *Lady Luck* would not stay afloat much longer, and we would go down with her.

Joen didn't say anything, she just stared, her emerald eyes piercing the dim light. I thought she would be angry with me, thought she deserved to be angry with me. We had parted in anger, and I had done nothing to apologize.

But there was no anger in her eyes. "Leave me," she said, "before it's too late."

I rose unsteadily. Could I abandon her to a watery fate? Could I leave her to die?

I looked at her again, long and hard, and sat back down.

Behind me, the door crashed open. I leaped to

my feet and turned to see the most beautiful sight imaginable.

"What're ye doin', Maimun?" said Tonnid. "Ship's gotta be abandoned, ye know?"

My mouth hung open, as dry as the Calim desert. So instead I pointed at Joen who had once again lifted her head from her hand and was slowly rising to her feet.

"Oh, uh," Tonnid stammered. "Well, that ain't good, is it?"

I started to answer, but Joen spoke first. "That'd depend on your perspective, eh?" There was a sharpness, a bitterness, in her voice.

"Who'd think it good ye're stuck in the cage?" Tonnid asked, patting himself all over with his hands. I thought he looked like he was trying to pat out some invisible flames, like Joen's words had somehow burned him.

"Oh, I don't know, maybe the one who put me here, eh?" Joen said.

"How can you say that!" I yelled. "I was following orders! I didn't want to lock you up!"

Joen turned to look at me, as if for the first time. "Oi, I wasn't talking about you, then. I meant your

R.A. & GENO SALVATORE

bloody captain, eh? I done nothing wrong, and he throws me in here like, like a . . ."

"Like a pirate," all three of us said at the same time.

"Look, maybe—" I began.

Tonnid gave a sudden shout. He was striding to the door, his hand held aloft, holding something small. Holding a key.

"Where did you get that, Tin?" I asked, my voice barely a whisper.

"Always have a a backup plan, ye know? Captain said I'd be the one he could trust with the spare, ye get it? In case something happens to the key."

Joen said what we both were thinking. "In case what happened, exactly?"

"Oh, I dunno, in case th' ship gets damaged, and the key falls out a hole in the wall, or something like that," he answered sarcastically. The cleverness of his joke astounded me; the one we called Tin-head had always been thought of as a decent man, and a good sailor, but never a particularly sharp thinker.

Of course, I could hardly make comparisons between me, the kid who had tried to free someone from the brig without a plan at all, and Tonnid, the man who had thought to bring a key.

The key clicked in the lock. The door fell open into the cage with a loud bang. The ship gave a mighty lurch.

And we three sailors ran for the deck.

CHAPTER TWENTY-ONE

Joen, Tonnid, and I cleared the hatch not a moment too soon.

Sea Sprite's teetering mast gave a final creak and ripped from the deck. Lines snapped as the towering pillar toppled sidelong into the water. The deck gave a mighty buck, the force that had held it at such a deep list being relieved. Like a pendulum it rocked back and forth, back and forth, all the while drifting out on the waves with the outgoing tide. And bringing us with it.

I ran across the deck, trying hard to keep my balance on the slick wood. Joen and Tonnid shambled along behind me. After many stumbles I reached the rail.

Lady Luck had sunk almost fully beneath the waves beside us. Only her sterncastle and her masts poked above the water, the fouled rigging still pulling *Sea Sprite* out to sea. Our own ship had not completely cleared the beach, but it would not be long. The lines which had been dropped to the beach dangled in the water.

I grasped one and swung a leg over the rail, but stopped halfway, stunned by the scene below.

On the beach, the crews of the two ships had divided and were facing each other, their weapons drawn. On one side, the crew of *Sea Sprite* stood in a fighting formation, their swords raised. On the other side, the crew of *Lady Luck*, sodden from their swim, held rocks, broken planks of wood, and whatever other makeshift weapons they had picked up on the beach. They stood clumped together, shivering, with no sort of battle formation and no captain to guide their battle. What appeared to be an attempt to create a campfire sat in front of them. But it remained unlit.

The crew of *Sea Sprite* advanced slowly, deliberately. I heard Captain Deudermont's voice. I could not hear the words, but I knew it would be a call to battle. It was with some surprise that I noted *Lady Luck*'s sailors bristling, moving forward, their primitive clubs at the ready.

"Why do they not throw down arms?" I asked Joen as she joined me at the rail.

She paused to take in the scene, then snarled an unintelligible answer and went over the side, landing with a splash.

"Wait!" I cried, leaping over the rail after her. I slipped off the rope but landed smoothly in the water, thanks to Perrault's ring.

Tonnid splashed down beside me. I rose, soaked, sympathizing with the crew of *Lady Luck*. But only for a moment.

Then I saw Joen sprinting off to join the pirates, scooping up a couple of rocks as she went.

I had nearly left her for dead in *Sea Sprite*'s brig just minutes before. I had nearly failed to save her. That would not happen again.

"Wait!" I called, running to the battle lines. "Captain, wait!"

I rushed forward, yelling all the way. Slowly, the sailors on each side saw me, and to a one they stopped in their tracks.

By the time I reached the center of the field, directly in front of Captain Deudermont, over a hundred people—every one of them older than I was, every one of them a more experienced sailor—were staring at me.

But would they listen?

Captain Deudermont's eyes were slit like daggers. "What is it?" he asked, his voice low.

"You have to stop this, Captain," I said.

Captain Deudermont looked very un-captainly in that moment. His clothes were torn and soaked. His face was drawn into a tight scowl, accentuated by a bloody cut on his left cheek. I had seen him angry before, but not such a rage, pure and simple.

"Once again, you dare question my orders," he spat.

I swallowed hard. "I'm sorry, sir, but you cannot do this," I said quietly. "This battle, it's wrong."

His eyes widened. "Wrong?" he said, his voice rising. "This crew destroyed my ship, killed my men, and we are the ones who are wrong? They deserve death, to a one."

The crew around him bristled, but only for a moment. Across the beach, *Lady Luck*'s crew advanced a few menacing steps, brandishing their weapons.

I waved frantically at them to stop. The last thing I wanted was a battle, and I knew one was coming if I did not quickly make my case. I grasped around in my thoughts, searching for a reason Deudermont should not kill all these people.

For a reason Joen should not die.

Joen should not have been among those pirates at all, I knew. She was not like them. And I could not allow her to be killed because of them. But there was no way I could bargain for her life and not the others, not after she had run to them though the battle lines were so clearly drawn.

"We fought them before, and you ordered them captured, not killed." I said at last, trying to keep my voice calm and reasonable. "What's changed?"

"They sank my ship!" Deudermont roared, and the crew of *Sea Sprite* cheered. A great crunch echoed in off the water as if to accentuate his point, as *Sea Sprite* collided with *Lady Luck* once more.

"We sank theirs first," I said, and the pirate crew roared in approval. I shot them a glare to silence them, but they paid me no heed.

"They sail out, pirates looking for plunder, and they attack us and they sink my ship. And we're in the wrong? You're a foolish child, foolish indeed, and I should never have let you on my crew! You're no better than they are, no better than a pirate yourself!"

"*Lady Luck* wasn't a pirate ship. She was a treasure hunter," I said. I felt bolstered by my own words, sure the captain would see my logic. "She was hunting a treasure that belongs to me. And I say we forgive her."

"Not a pirate ship?" Deudermont snarled. "You yourself named their captain as a pirate."

I pointed to the clump of pirates. "But the captain is not among them now."

Deudermont stepped toward me. "I don't care where their captain is. When he ordered the attack on us, his crew became our enemy. Every one of them."

Including Joen. I felt myself deflate, felt my argument falling apart.

Captain Deudermont glared at me. "I will not tolerate any more of this insubordination from you, Mister Maimun." He motioned to the crew assembled beside him, and the one across the beach. "Choose your side."

I stared down at the sand. If only Joen hadn't run from me. We could have stayed out of the fight. No one would have faulted us. Surely Captain Deudermont would have spared Joen's life then.

But she had chosen to side with the pirates to the death. And I was powerless to stop it.

I felt a hand on my shoulder, and at first I thought I was imagining it. I turned to face Joen, standing beside me before the captain.

"Our captain did not order an attack on your ship, sir," she said. Her voice was quiet. "You fired first."

"She's right!" I stared up at him. "The first shot was from our catapult!"

"A warning shot," he replied. "Which your captain did not heed. Your wizard attacked us from your deck. Or did he not count because he isn't here either?" Deudermont was taunting me. I felt my face flush red with hot anger.

"Look, sir," said Joen quite calmly. "I know you're angry. You want revenge. But what good is revenge now? This storm's sunk both our ships."

As she said that, a great form darkened the seaward sky. The hull of our ship, with its mast ripped up and laying on deck, slid ashore with surprisingly little noise.

"Well, it sunk one ship then, eh? The other it just broke and beached." Joen chuckled. She always managed to find the humor in the darkest of situations.

"There's no way your crew could repair your ship after fighting the rest of us," Joen went on. "You've not enough men. And your crew's already injured as it is."

The storm seemed to feel the mood changing. The wind howled a little less loudly; the sleet slowed to an icy drizzle. The dark sky on the edge of the horizon revealed a lighter patch where the sun was trying to poke its light through.

"What are you proposing?" Deudermont asked. The rage had not entirely left his voice, but it had surely lessened. Slowly, his sword arm fell to his side.

"We help you repair your ship, you give us a ride back to Waterdeep, eh?" Joen stepped closer to Deudermont. "No charges, no trial, nothing. We want to go home."

Deudermont was shaking his head. The idea of letting the pirates go surely did not settle well with him. But he could not argue with Joen's logic. He needed every man on the beach. If he did not accept their help, we were all doomed.

The clouds blew off the we[st] enough to reveal a sliver of golde[n] danced about in the setting sun, b[...] light, near the top of the short h[ill] center of the island.

With a start, I realized the[y] turned and flew closer, until th[...] on the sand.

My blood ran cold as they f[...] wings touching. All nine stared [at] me, only at me.

And then they were not rav[ens]

Where the birds had stood [...] wearing billowing black robes [...] by shadowmasks.

Chapter Twenty-Two

"We are not here to harm you," said the man closest to me. "We come with a message. Which is the captain?"

Deudermont did not hesitate, but strode up right before the speaker, unblinking. "I am the captain," he said. "And I am not in the habit of talking to men in masks."

"Talking will not be necessary," the man replied. "Only listening. We have brought you here for a reason."

"Brought us here?" Deudermont said. "We crashed here in a storm!"

"You said you did not want to talk," said the masked man.

"And we agreed with you," said the one to his right.

"The storm brought you here, yes," said the next in line, that one a woman.

"But we controlled the storm," said another man. I was paying more attention to their voices than to their words, listening for a specific voice, the one I had heard in Memnon. The voice of the woman who had stolen the stone from me.

"We have brought you here for a reason," repeated the man who had first spoken, apparently the leader. "You have among you a treasure we must protect."

"What treasure?" Deudermont sounded unconvinced.

"A child."

"No children on my ship."

In unison, the nine robed figures all cocked their heads to the side, a curious expression made all the more odd by the expressionless masks they wore.

"A young man, then," said the leader. He motioned to me. "He led you out here, or for his sake you came. We know you would not dare brave these waters in such weather, Captain."

R.A. & GENO SALVATORE

"We came following another ship," Deudermont said defensively.

"Yes, and now you are both wrecked and trapped here. So let us be done with the fencing. You have the boy. We want the boy. We will not let you leave with him. You may stay as long as you like. But be warned there is not enough food for the lot of you. Or you may leave without him. But he may not leave the island."

Deudermont puffed up his chest. "I am Captain Deudermont of the good ship *Sea Sprite*, commissioned by the Lords of Waterdeep. I do not need your permission to do anything." With that, he spun on his heel and turned his back on the strangers.

"Captain Deudermont, however good your ship may be, she still needs a fair wind. As we have said, we can give or deny that wind." As he finished, the wind gusted once, mightily, the robes of the nine whipping around in fury.

Then, suddenly and completely, it stopped.

The whole of the island seemed to have fallen into silence. The only sound was the waves, lapping gently against the shore. They were peaceful and serene, so unlike the wind-whipped breakers of but moments earlier.

THE *SHADOWMASK*

Deudermont slowly turned back to face the robed figures. But he did not look at them. He stared into the distance, as if looking right past them. "Who are you?" he whispered. "And what do you want?"

"We are simply called the Circle," replied the leader. "And we exist, like many of our brother and sister Circles, to maintain the balance of a region. And these past dozen years, the balance of your Sword Coast has been failing. We will keep the boy here, so that balance can be maintained."

Captain Deudermont did not appear to be listening at all; he just continued to stare into the sunset behind the robed man, the leader of the Circle. I knew the captain was angry with me, but I was sure he wouldn't be so cruel as to abandon me to those thieves. Not after everything I'd been through—after everything we'd been through together.

After a long pause, Deudermont turned to his crew, his face calm. "Let's get some fires burning. Dry off, warm up." He put his hand on Joen's shoulder. "Tomorrow we work, pirates and sailors alike. We fix *Sea Sprite*, and we sail back to Waterdeep." Then he fixed his gaze on me. "Without you."

I stood, my mouth agape, unable to believe what

I was hearing. But Captain Deudermont ignored me, and he walked away up the beach.

The pirates cheered as they followed Deudermont. The crew of *Sea Sprite* slumped after them.

Only one remained.

I stepped toward Joen, my hand reaching out for her.

Her hair fell around her eyes, concealing her expression. After a moment, she turned away from me and followed the rest of the crowd to the shore.

The last sliver of the sun disappeared behind the island, and the mysterious Circle vanished with it, as suddenly and as completely as if they were flames on a candle that had just been blown out.

Part Three

THE SHADOWMASK

A few moments passed before the pirate noticed I was no longer talking. I stared at him, and he stared back at me.

"Well?" he finally asked.

"I told you not to interrupt me," I said lightly.

"I didn't interrupt ye! Ye just stopped!" he snapped.

I laughed a little; he seemed none too pleased. "I was just testing something," I told him.

"Testing? Whaddya mean?"

"I wanted to see how long you'd wait before interrupting the story."

He snarled and rose to his feet. "I didn't interrupt, ye fool boy. Now quit yer mocking and get on with the tale!"

"Not just yet," I said. "First we have to settle something."

His hand dropped to his sword, and he started to speak, but I cut him off.

"I know you aren't going to kill me. Don't bother with the sword, it's getting old."

"It's getting old, like ye ne'er will," he

said. He advanced a step and pulled out his cutlass. "And what makes ye think I ain't gonna gut ye right here?"

"You want to know where the story goes," I said, keeping my eyes fixed on his simmering ones.

"I know where it goes," he said with a half-snarl, half-laugh. "It goes right here, to this li'l cave on this li'l isle."

"You know where it ends," I corrected him. "But you want to know where it goes. You want to know what happens between that island and this one. And if you kill me, you'll never find out."

He stood there, glowering at me, for a long while. I kept my gaze locked with his the whole time, watched as the rage in his eyes died just a little, his stare softened just a bit.

"What did ye wan' to settle, then?" he asked.

I smiled at him; he did not return the gesture. "I need a few things from you if we are to continue. First, I need food."

"Ye've been fed," he snarled.

"Barely, and at your leisure. I want full meals. Second, I want a light. A lantern or a torch, and the means to keep it burning."

He pointed to the torch in the sconce on the wall. "Alright, so I be leaving the torch when I go, an' I get ye something ter eat, an' ye'll finish yer tale?" He did well to mask it, but I heard the slightest hint of relief, of contentment, in his voice. He really did want to hear the rest, and my demands apparently seemed reasonable to him.

But I had one more demand. "Third," I said, "and last, I need your word."

He blinked a few times, apparently not comprehending what I was asking. "Me word on what?"

"That when I finish my story, you will not kill me."

He laughed uproariously, a rolling belly laugh that stretched on for what seemed like minutes. Each time he paused to catch his breath, and opened his mouth to speak, another bout of laughter came pouring out. I half expected some of the other pirates to hear him and come to investigate, but after a few minutes none had arrived, and he finally managed to speak.

"Me word ye can have," he said. "But ye know the score: a word's only as good as the man giving it. An' I ain't a good man!"

"No, you aren't," I said, prompting another burst of laughter. "But Captain Deudermont, he is a good man. And I've seen him break his own word. So I put little value in anyone's word, good or bad."

"Then what do ye want me word fer?" he asked.

"I asked you before not to interrupt me, and you didn't. So you can keep your promises. I'll choose to believe you when you say you won't kill me."

"A bold choice."

"Perhaps," I said, smiling mysteriously. "But I think you'll see how it will pay off—for both of us—in the end."

CHAPTER TWENTY-THREE

Lightning flashed in the sky overhead, accompanied by the thunderous snores of the crewmen sleeping around the campsite. We had salvaged what we could of the dried foodstuffs from *Sea Sprite*'s hold, and my belly was pleasantly full. I had managed to retrieve my pack from the hold as well, and I tucked it under my head as a makeshift pillow. The night sky was clear, and though the air was still cold, the fire kept me warm, especially with Perrault's magical cloak wrapped tightly around me.

Still, I slept poorly that night. Perrault danced across my vision, sometimes alone, sometimes arm in arm with the woman in the obsidian mask. Dark shapes circled above us—ravens keeping watch over their prize. Again and again flashes of light filled the sky, each illuminating a different scene. I wavered in and out of sleep, and I could not tell what was real and what was dream.

But awake or asleep, I felt the same unease.

None of *Sea Sprite*'s crew would even look at me. They could not bear the guilt, I figured, knowing they were abandoning me. Joen had returned to her crew and slept among them several yards up the shoreline, at a campfire of their own. She had not spoken another word to me, and I did not dare approach her.

Sea Sprite had not even left the island. And already I was all alone.

My eyes flew open. I pulled myself to my feet, and I began walking down the beach.

I didn't know where I would go. But I couldn't stand waiting any longer. Soon the crews would begin to rebuild the ship so they could sail out to sea, without me. I could help with the repairs, perhaps, but would they even want me near them? And even if they did, why should I help them?

I felt my anger rising. It pushed my legs faster, quickened my pace until I broke into a jog.

I skirted the shoreline, just at the water's edge, my bare feet kicking up icy spray with every step. The beach was dotted with small fading campfires, with everyone around them peacefully asleep. I came to the edge of the camp, where flames roared around a large pile of driftwood. I saw Captain Deudermont, Robillard, and a few of *Sea Sprite*'s men, fast asleep.

I ducked my head, hoping none would waken as I passed. I could not bear to look at Deudermont's face, even his sleeping face. My mind rolled through all the interactions I'd had with the captain over the past months: the first meeting, where he had offered me a job on his ship. Calimport, where he had agreed to help me find a certain dark elf. Waterdeep, where he had agreed, against his wishes, to sail into the wintry sea on my hunch. He had always seemed so genuinely friendly, if a bit distant. I thought I could trust him. But he had betrayed me.

Just like every one of my fellow crew members. My hands curled into fists as I pushed harder down the beach. When the Circle presented their terms, had any of my crew stood up for me? They had stood there in silence. They would rather just leave me to my fate.

I rounded a rocky spur to find another open stretch of beach. Large blubbery walruses, grey-furred, with broad flippers and tusks as long as my arm lounged there, sleeping quietly. Any of them could surely have killed me, or at least hurt me badly, but in my anger I didn't care.

I picked my way through the crowd of the great beasts—there must have been several hundred of them, each longer than I was tall, and probably half a ton apiece.

In the darkness I couldn't help but step on a flipper every so often. But even when I did, the walruses didn't seem to notice, too content in their dreams to waken.

Content, like the crew back at the camp. Even the crew of *Lady Luck* slept soundly, knowing they would soon be heading home. Didn't they owe me a debt of gratitude? I thought bitterly. Had I not been the one who negotiated with Deudermont, to allow them passage home instead of slaughtering them all on that field? Yet none of them had stood up for me, either. None of them had shown the slightest recognition of what Joen and I had done for them.

Joen . . .

My mind flashed red with pure anger too primal to put into words. I let out a roar, a scream of hate and anguish that I hoped would echo all the way back to the camp, where she would hear it and know what I felt.

All it did was rouse the walruses around me. They responded with roars of their own, great barking noises like some perverse giant dog with a sore throat.

One barked out above all the others, a ferocious sound that made my blood freeze in my veins. The commotion died instantly. The walruses settled. Except that those nearest me shifted away, forming a clear path to the largest of them all, who was slowly moving toward me. It moved like a man wounded in the legs, I thought, pulling itself forward on its front flippers, its tail dragging behind him. But it was not graceless—far from it: the creature had practiced that movement for decades, I knew. It was in complete control of its body, unwieldy and massive though it was. Its great tusked and whiskered head bobbed up and down as it approached. Each time its head rose, it issued a bark. It growled each time its head fell.

It had to be the pack's leader, I thought. Like the wolves of my childhood in the High Forest, the walruses must fight each other to determine who would stand as the greatest of the group. That bull showed the signs of many battles—its left tusk was cracked, its tip splintered away. Its body was not a solid gray, like most of the others, but was streaked with scars. And the worst of the scars crossed his face, just below his right eye—a great patch of black on its wrinkled, ancient face.

It was barking a challenge, I realized. I was an intruder, a threat, and it was demanding that I face it in combat or surrender. The choice was not a difficult one, given that it was no less than ten times my weight, with a thick hide and vicious weapons.

I bent low to the ground in a sort of bow, lowering my head deferentially, and retreated a few shuffling steps.

It stopped for a moment, staring at me, then raised its head in what I took to be a victorious motion, and let out a long roar. The crowd of walruses joined in, bobbing their heads and barking a deafening chorus. I kept my head down and slowly backed through the crowd and out onto the clear beach beyond.

"You always were so good with animals," said a quiet voice behind me, a voice I recognized.

I spun around, pulling my stiletto from its sheath, to face the masked woman I had met in Memnon.

But she was no longer masked. And even in the dim light of the half moon, I saw her face clearly. My dagger fell from my hand, thudding softly on the sand.

My mind whirled back across the years, back to my earliest childhood. Back to a small cave in an ancient forest, to the summer nights beneath the boughs, to the forest animals, to the only time in my life I had ever stayed in one place longer than a few months.

To the first time I had met Asbeel, that dark midsummer night. To the bolt of lightning, guided by a friendly hand into my cave, to scare off the demon.

To the fires in the forest. To the last time I had ever seen the only mother I had ever known.

"You died," I whispered.

Elbeth shook her head slowly, wearing the slightest of smiles on her ageless face. "You've grown," she said quietly.

"Tried not to; didn't work." I shrugged.

She laughed slightly. "I've watched you from afar, but I hadn't realized how strong you've become."

"I can't believe you're here." I rushed forward and buried my head in her arms.

But after only a moment, she pulled away. "We haven't much time, child," she said, glancing quickly over her shoulder. "I must leave soon."

"Leave? Why?" I asked. The growl that escaped my lips did not seem my own. My anger had a new target, and it was right before me.

Elbeth sighed. "I do what has to be done, child. As I ever have."

"What has to be done?" I took a step back. "You had to let a five-year-old boy think his mother had died?"

"I am not your mother."

"You were close enough!"

Elbeth gave me a curious look. I swallowed. Was what she had been close enough? I had had a real mother, after all. And a real father too. What would life have been like if they had not died? If I had never gone to live in the forest with Elbeth? I took in a breath as a new thought crossed my mind.

"Did they really die?" I asked quietly.

Elbeth nodded, and I knew she understood whom I was talking about.

"I never hated them for it." I sighed and stared at the sand. "And I never hated you for dying, either." I looked back at her, my eyes filling with tears.

"But now how can I not hate you, now that I know the truth?"

"You can hate me as much as you want. But I didn't abandon you, truly, did I? I left you with Perrault."

"You left me *for* Perrault," I corrected. "And hoped he would find me."

She shook her head. "Perrault had found you once before, lying beside your murdered mother. I made certain that he would find you again." Elbeth stepped forward and took my chin in her hand. "Tell me, child. Do you regret your time with him?"

The memories were painful, but I could not keep them from coming. Perrault had shown me the mountains, the great rivers, forests nestled in snowy valleys, and oases in arid deserts. With him I had seen much of western Faerûn, wonders no child my age could hope to witness.

And the stories, told and read, of battles won and lost and legends of old. Dragons buried beneath the hills, monsters slain on the top of mountains, and true heroes journeying into the fires of the Abyss.

And all that still could not begin to describe what Perrault had meant to me, the person behind the stories and the journeys. He had never been very

THE *SHADOWMASK*

warm, but he had always been there, always guiding me. Whenever I had a question, Perrault would not answer directly but would lead me through a series of other questions, showing me the way to the answer.

Elbeth stood before me, a look of the deepest understanding on her face.

"I can't regret Perrault," I said at last. "But why couldn't he have lived with us, in the forest?"

She laughed. "Perrault, hidden away in a forest? Perhaps he could have, but never would he have!"

"Then why couldn't you have traveled with us?" I asked.

She shook her head. "Your time with Perrault was special because it was you and him."

I swallowed. "He's dead too, now, you know."

She took my hand and squeezed it. "We have spoken enough of the past. We have more immediate matters to discuss. I'm sure you are wondering why we are here."

I nodded, my mind still reeling at the sight of her.

"I am here," she said, "because my duties have brought me here, to join this Circle for the time being. You are here because the stone you are bound to is here."

I felt like she had punched me in the gut. "The stone is here?"

"Haven't you felt better as you grew closer? The illness that had afflicted you since your separation—isn't it gone?"

Reflexively, I flexed my left hand. Indeed the numbness that had crippled me had faded the moment we set sail to the west, heading toward the island. It was just a vague memory.

"When we took the stone from you, we did not know how you would react. We hoped you would suffer no physical ailment, if only we brought the stone far enough from you."

"When you stole the stone, you mean," I said.

"I volunteered for that, child. Because I knew I could not only get the stone, but could prevent the others who sought it from harming you. And I was correct, as it turns out."

"I could have fought Asbeel." I would not concede that she'd helped me at all. Elbeth had stolen the stone. All I could think of was that betrayal. She had betrayed me just like everyone else. "I didn't need your help."

"Be not such a fool. The demon would have killed you."

"So you saved me from him," I said sarcastically, "then took the stone from me. And being away from the stone caused illness. So you almost killed me anyway."

"I am sorry for that." She put her hand on my shoulder. "I know now it was a mistake. But then it was not my decision to give you the stone in the first place."

"Don't try to put this on him!" I yelled and shrugged away her hand. A chorus of barks erupted behind me again.

"I am not. But think back. Would things not have been better had you never touched the stone?"

"Perrault said I was old enough to have back what was mine." I glared at her. "The stone is my birth-right. He said it was tied to me already."

"I believe that things could have turned out differently." She looked behind me at the distant waves. "Your soul grows full as you mature. It may well have scarred over the missing part where the stone should have been." She sighed and turned back to meet my gaze. "But now I realize, it's too late. All we know is you can't be separated from it, or else you will fall terribly ill. That is why I insisted the Circle bring you here, where you will be near it again."

"You brought me back here to keep me near the stone," I said. "As a prisoner."

"That was the Circle's goal, yes."

"But why?"

"The story is far too long to explain." Elbeth glanced quickly over her shoulder. "And I mustn't be gone for much longer, or they will start to suspect. Suffice it to say if Tymora's stone is active, at this time, on Toril, then it creates a great imbalance. Good luck for one means bad for another, and the stone had given you undue luck. The circle exists to prevent such imbalances."

"So I have to suffer in the name of balance? That hardly seems fair."

"It is not indeed. But, as I said, it is the Circle's goal."

"The Circle's goal," I repeated. I looked deep into her eyes. "But not yours?"

She shook her head solemnly. "The Circle intends to keep you prisoner. But I cannot bear to see you held against your will. I know now this is not your fate." She spoke faster, her voice a low growl. "The stone is hidden in a cave. The cave lies beneath the water there," she said, pointing at the rocky outcropping at the end of the beach, back toward the sailors' camp. "At low tide, the cave will be exposed."

I looked at her, my eyes wide. "So you want me to go in and steal the stone? Why can't you just give it back to me?"

"It is not my place to return it to you," she said. "But since the stone belongs to you, your taking it is not theft." She took in a deep breath. "I must warn you, this task is not simple. A great guardian of the sea lives in that cave. Be careful that you do not wake him. Even goodly dragons are cranky when they wake, especially if they wake to find a thief in their den."

I barely heard a word past "dragon." My head was spinning. I had always been most fascinated by tales of dragons, the rarest and mightiest of the creatures of the Realms. I found them brilliant and awe-inspiring and ultimately deadly and had always hoped to see one some day. But under these particular circumstances?

"Wait until the ship is repaired," Elbeth continued, not oblivious to my suddenly wobbly knees. "Get the stone, and get back to the ship just as it pushes out to sea."

"What about the Circle?" I asked. "What about Deudermont? He said he—"

Elbeth waved her hand in front of me. "You need not worry about Deudermont. You have a place on his ship. And I will take care of the Circle to give you enough time to escape."

"You'll stop them one against eight?" I asked.

"For as long as I can," she said. She gave me a wide, warm smile. "Which may not be long at all."

"And then what?"

Elbeth picked up my fallen dagger and pressed it into my hand. "You must find a way to restore the balance."

I nodded, trying to think of something to say. The whole plan sounded very dangerous for both of us, but I could think of no better alternative. I had no intention of staying on the island for the rest of my life, certainly not in the name of preserving some mystical balance. So I would face the dragon, and she would face her compatriots, and we would have to hope for the best.

With a heavy heart, I turned and began the long walk back to the camp.

"Who is she?" Elbeth called after me, her voice

light, almost happy, despite the gravity of the plan we'd just laid.

"Who is who?" I asked, turning back to face her.

"The girl, the blonde," she said. "She followed you out of the camp, you know, but got spooked by the walruses. She's awake, waiting for you, right now."

I opened my mouth to respond, but nothing came out. I turned on my heel and sprinted off as fast as I could.

"Going?" I said.

She punched me in the arm, not hard, but enough to leave a bruise. I pulled away, and she followed, a wicked grin on her face, her hand cocked for another punch.

"Stop, stop!" I said, laughing, surprised that I could manage a laugh. "You aren't mad, and you aren't going mad either. It was magic, I think. I've seen it used before."

"Figured as much. I ain't crazy, you know? But who was it?"

Of course it had been Elbeth. That's why she hadn't spoken when the Circle presented their demands to Deudermont. She had been whispering a message on the wind, her face hidden behind her mask.

Suddenly I remembered Deudermont's vacant stare, as if he weren't listening to the leader of the Circle at all. Could it be that Elbeth had sent him a message as well?

"Well?" Joen asked impatiently. "You gonna tell me who it was, or do I have to beat it out of you?" She cocked her arm and balled her fist.

"It was a friend," I said. "She's going to help me escape, but I have to do something first."

"Oi, how original," Joen said, rolling her eyes. "What's she makin' you do?"

"It's not for her," I said, considering how much I could tell Joen. "The Circle stole something from me, and she told me where it's hidden."

"Great. So, we wait 'til the repairs are done, then we go get it, eh?"

"We?"

"You're only telling me 'cause you want me to come with. Don't deny it, you know it's true too."

I hesitated. "It's too dangerous," I said.

"All the more reason I should come. Someone's gotta have your back."

"Would you have had my back out on the beach, if you hadn't heard the whisper?" I tried, but failed, to keep accusation out of my voice.

She reached out and grasped my hand in hers. I turned to face her directly, to look straight into her emerald eyes, shining in the dim light. I felt suddenly guilty for questioning her, for ever being angry with her. My palm grew sweaty in her strong grasp. There was so little distance between us, so little . . .

The hatch above swung open. We dropped our hands.

A voice called down: "Lunch at the campsite. Make yer way to the shore!"

Joen skipped lightly for the ladder, not once looking over her shoulder at me. I waited a long moment, replaying our conversation in my head, before I started off for the lunch table.

CHAPTER TWENTY-FIVE

The days passed slowly, filled as they were with hard work, poor shelter, and worse food. The weather stayed calm and relatively warm—the sun shone by day and the moon grew toward full, illuminating the night. Each evening Robillard would magically start new fires to keep us warm, and we would settle down to sleep. Deudermont posted a watch, unnecessary though it seemed. Certainly no external threat would rear its head, and it seemed unlikely to me that the crew of *Lady Luck* would try to cause any trouble.

Still, the two crews slept apart, each around their own fires. Joen remained loyal to her ship and slept among them. I still considered most of them pirates, evil men who would hurt me given the chance, so I avoided them.

But during the days we often found ourselves alone in the hold, sifting through the waterlogged supplies for anything useful. During high tide, we sat on the beach with the few crewmen who were still injured, since none of us were much use with the manual labor on board.

We talked about the past—about both our pasts. She told me of her parents, who died when she was young. She grew up in Luskan, alone on the streets, making her own way by picking pockets. When she turned nine, she took on with a ship, posing as a boy that she might be offered a job as cabin boy. I told her about my own past, from Elbeth to the present, mostly truthfully. I glossed over some parts, in particular not telling her that Elbeth was on the island.

We only occasionally discussed our plan. After all, it was very simple in theory: on the day *Sea Sprite* was ready to sail, we would go to the cave, take the stone, run back to the ship, and leave. But something still worried me.

Late on the night of the sixth day, I jostled Joen awake.

"Joen, I need to tell you something," I said. The sun had long since set; the midnight hour was past.

"Later," she said, closing her eyes and rolling over. "I'm busy."

"It's about the mission," I said, keeping my voice hushed. "When we get there, you can't go into the cave."

"Haven't we been over this, then?" She lifted herself onto her elbows and peered up at me. "It's dangerous, it's something you have to do, blah blah. I told you: you need someone to watch your back, and that's me."

"It's too dangerous."

She rolled her eyes at me. "You don't listen, do you? I know it's dangerous, I'm coming anyway. What is it, anyway, a dragon or something?"

She laughed, but I did not join her. After a moment she caught my solemn expression and stared at me in disbelief.

"Seriously?" she asked, her voice a hushed whisper.

I nodded.

She looked at me long and hard, her mouth slightly open. I figured she was trying to read my face, to know that I was telling the truth. After a moment, though, her lips curled into that smile again.

"I've always wanted to see a dragon," she said lightly. "This should be fun, eh?"

"Fun?" I said in disbelief. "Are you insane?"

"Maybe," she said, smiling. "But what's the worst that could happen?"

Images of her tiny corpse danced through my mind, ripped to shreds, charred to ash. I could not express in words what I saw, the worst that could happen. But I did not argue.

"That's settled then, eh?" She flopped back down and pulled her blanket over her head. "Now leave me alone."

On the seventh day, the mast had been reset and the deck around it rebuilt, and it was time to start resetting the rigging. Suddenly Joen and I found ourselves the most-worked members of the crew, as we were the two best able to get to the very top of the mast or the farthest out on the wings above the sails. We had no time to talk, and when our long days ended we were both so exhausted we would go to sleep without any words exchanged.

Then finally on the tenth day, the last lines were tied, and Captain Deudermont declared *Sea Sprite* to be seaworthy. The tide was going out, so she was mostly on the beach. At the next high tide, the crew would put her in the water, then be off as the waves began to recede.

It was time.

An hour before dawn, I quietly packed my gear and slipped into my boots—the magical boots that Sali Dalib had "loaned" me what seemed like a thousand years before. Careful not to wake anyone, I snuck out of camp, alone. The lookouts weren't paying much attention—as usual—so it was easy to get out unseen. But I wanted to take every precaution anyway. Not long after, Joen came skipping up the beach.

Her hair was pale in the moonlight. It almost shimmered as it bounced up and down in time with her skip. She was heading off to her doom, to face a dragon, to steal from a dragon, and she was doing so with a light step and a smile on her face.

Perhaps I had been wrong before; perhaps she was indeed insane.

But was I any less crazy?

All too soon, the rocky outcropping where Elbeth said the cave would be was right in front of us.

It was a two-tiered natural rock formation. A stone cliff rose perhaps twenty feet up on the left. A similar face dropped another ten feet to the right. A narrow path snaked between the two. At high tide, the lower rock would be completely covered by the sea. But the tide was nearly out, and fully seven feet of dark, jagged rock was clearly visible. The jags made fine handholds, and I had no trouble at all climbing down. The water was still several feet deep at the base, but just above the lapping waves I saw a dark slit—the top of a cave.

"What do you see?" Joen called down.

"We're gonna have to get wet," I yelled back.

"Oi, on with it, then," she said, pulling herself over the lip and starting the short climb down.

I blew a sigh under my breath, wishing I could gather the courage to tell her, once and for all, that she could not come in, that I could not let her risk her own safety for my sake. But I had no such courage, so I dropped into the water instead.

I paddled forward. From my vantage point the whole mouth of the cave was visible. I drew out my stiletto, ignited the blue flame, and held it into the opening; just past the cave mouth, a narrow tunnel sloped upward. I swam for the edge, and scrambled out, happy to be out of the ice-cold water.

A splash behind me told me Joen had dropped into the water, and she quickly joined me in the cave. Together we slipped into the tunnel.

The roof scraped against my back, though I crawled flat on my belly. The rocks were wet and slick for the first dozen yards, but they rose steadily, soon clearing the highest water levels of high tide. The air there was much warmer—a blessing: my wet clothes would not freeze.

The tunnel flattened out and gained enough height that we could walk upright. I tried to illuminate the ground in front of us, but the light cast by my flaming stiletto was meager, and many times each we tripped over a jag or a crack in the stone passage.

We walked for what seemed like an hour in silence before the landscape changed. There was no gradual widening of the tunnel, no growth of the cave into a cavern. All of a sudden, the walls and ceiling just disappeared, stretching out around a massive chamber. My light seemed tiny indeed, a pinprick of blue on a great black tapestry.

I thought I heard a sound: a low rumble, rhythmic, and slow. I held out my hand. "Wait!" I whispered. "I think I hear something."

But after a few moments of standing there, I felt only a deep dark silence.

"Don't be a baby. The dragon's out hunting or fast asleep." Joen pushed my shoulder. "On with it, eh?"

Not wanting to seem the coward, I stepped deliberately into the cavern, one step, two, three . . . I saw a glint ahead and moved toward it.

Suddenly the darkness was gone. The light from my magical dagger caught the thing I had seen ahead: a strange sphere with many glassy mirrored facets. The sphere seemed to grab at the light, then project it out from each of those mirrors, amplified ten times over. The whole of the room filled with a pale blue glow.

With my heart in my throat, I quickly scanned the room. There were piles of gold coins, sapphires and emeralds, silver necklaces dotted with rubies. Shortswords and longswords and scale armor, masterfully crafted and probably enchanted. Against one wall stood what looked like an ancient desk and delicately carved bookshelves, filled with leather bound books and scrolls and vials of blue and green liquid.

But I could see no sign of a dragon.

I blew out a low sigh. Joen skipped past me, smiling broadly, practically dancing her way into the treasure. She bent low to scoop up a handful of coins, then let most of it trickle through her fingers as she laughed. A few coins she pocketed, then made to repeat the action.

"No," I whispered harshly. "We're here for something specific, remember?"

"Oi, right, sure," she said, still staring at the coins. "What's it look like, then?"

"It's a leather sash with a large pouch on the front," I said. "The pouch should hold something heavy."

"Right," she said. "We should split the search. You go that way,"—she pointed to the wall with the books and magical equipment—"and I'll go this way." She moved off into the largest piles of treasure, giggling like the silly girl I knew she wasn't.

I moved off toward the wall, not wanting to argue. Besides, the stone could well be that way, and even if it wasn't, I wouldn't mind a chance to look through the ancient books. I had just picked one up when I heard Joen call out to me.

"Oi, this it, then?" she said, and I looked back to see her holding up a leather sash—my leather sash.

"That's it!" I called. "Is the stone in it?"

"Some kind of stone, yeah. Big and black. That's what you're after, eh? The stone?"

"That's right," I said, walking toward her. I had hated the burden of the stone when I had carried it, but all I could think about was holding it again.

"Oi, and look at this!" she shrieked, holding up a jewel-studded belt. "Was lying there, right next to yours! And look, it's got some matching knives on it too. I could use a new pair, you know, ever since your captain took mine."

"Put it back," I said forcefully.

"What, you get to steal from the dragon but I don't?"

"I'm not stealing. I'm reclaiming what's mine."

"You think he's gonna see it that way?" Defiantly, she strapped the belt to her waist. "What, he shows up you gonna say, 'hey mister dragon, this was mine before, I'm just taking it back,' and he's gonna let you go?"

"No," growled a voice, deep as thunder and echoing about the cave endlessly. "I will not."

"But a liar, you admit to?" the beast said. I had no idea dragons could laugh, but it seemed to be laughing at me.

"No, because the stone is mine to reclaim," I said. Behind the dragon, Joen finally snapped from her stupor and began to pick her way down the loose slope of coins, careful not to make a sound. "If the Circle hadn't told me where to find the stone, how would I have known to come here?"

The dragon blinked for the first time, staring at me curiously. "That may be so," it said, sounding unsure. I got the distinct impression it was trying to sort through the circumstances that had brought the stone to its possession.

"It is!" I said. "The Circle stole the stone from me. And now they want me to have it back. I am here to reclaim what is rightfully mine." Joen had reached the base of the pile, and was moving quickly to the narrow cave entrance we'd used to enter.

The dragon sniffed at the air, its eyes growing wide. "Thieves!" it bellowed. "Thieves and liars! You'll not leave this place, fools!" Its head shot around to where Joen had been standing, crashing against the pile, sending gold and silver and gems flying everywhere.

I took off running, racing Joen to the exit. Sali Dalib's boots hastened my step, but I wasn't quite fast enough. The dragon's head turned on me once again, and I heard the beast's sharp intake of breath. I reached the tunnel just as it exhaled.

The air around me tingled with energy, an electric charge building for just one brief moment. Something slammed against my back, with the force of a thunder-stroke and a sound to match. I flew through the air, crashing against Joen. We both tumbled into the narrow passage.

She scrambled to her feet, half-sobbing, her limp hand around my arm. I pulled myself up beside her, bruised but mostly unhurt. The look on her face was a mix of horror and confusion.

"You . . ." she whispered, her voice quivering. "Your . . ." I thought I saw a tear drip down her cheek, but she brushed it aside and shook her head vigor-ously. "Your cloak," she said, her voice normal again. "It looks a bit worse for the wear, eh?"

I pulled my cloak over my shoulder. Indeed it looked worse: the brilliant royal blue was marked with a great black scar, with small red veins running the length of it.

An image of Perrault leaped into my mind: galloping atop his white steed Haze with the cloak flowing out behind him.

I shook my head, trying to suppress the sick feeling in my gut. "No time to waste, we have to move," I said.

It had seemed an hour getting to the treasure. But it felt like a mere minute before we were crawling down the narrow sloped tunnel toward freedom. Somewhere along the way, I had taken the sash from Joen and placed it over my head. Though it was on top of my shirt, not under it as I used to wear it, its familiar weight felt good against my chest. It was like it was inside my chest, inside my very being. Even through the illness it had caused, I had not noticed how much I had missed the stone until the moment I finally had it back.

We scrambled out of the cave into the predawn light. The tide had gone out further, and there was less than a foot of water beneath out feet. We stopped to catch our breath before starting the short climb and long walk back to the camp.

"How do you suppose the dragon got in there?" Joen asked me. "You think it crawled in when it was tiny, and just outgrew the entrance?"

"Then how would it have all that treasure?" I said. "And what did it eat to grow so large?"

"I dunno, maybe the Circle feeds it and brings it gifts." She shrugged.

"Or maybe there's another, larger, entrance," I said.

Her response was cut short by a loud splashing noise. A few hundred yards out to sea, the water bubbled, and a great reptilian head emerged, followed by the rest of the dragon, wings spread wide, a hundred feet long, wingspan twice that across.

It let loose a roar so loud the rock shook beneath our feet. The mighty beast beat its wings against the air, and turned to the shore—to us.

"Time to go," I said quietly. But Joen was no longer standing beside me; she was halfway up the cliff and climbing fast.

I followed her, quick as I could, thankful for the easy handholds. My palms were sweaty, and my fingers trembled. I doubted I could have navigated a more difficult cliff.

When I crested the rise, my heart beat even faster.

Joen stood, her daggers drawn, her feet set in a defensive stance. Behind her stood a figure with black boots and pants and a white silk shirt stretched over a broad red chest. The twisted metal hilt of a horrible demonic sword rose up beside the wicked, angular face.

"Impressive," Asbeel said with feigned friendliness. "I half expected you'd never return from that cave. Then again, you did have some luck,"—he looked pointedly at the sash across my chest—"on your side."

CHAPTER TWENTY-SEVEN

One, two, three times I slashed at Asbeel, left to right. After all that training with the masters of Waterdeep, my swordwork had vastly improved since the last time Asbeel and I had crossed swords. But against Asbeel, it didn't seem to make much difference.

Each time, I struck out at him, his own massive sword was in line for the block.

Joen crouched low to my right. Her heels dangled off the cliff, as she stabbed out with her newly stolen daggers.

Asbeel brought his sword around quickly, aiming a swing at her head. But Joen darted to her left.

I stepped forward, my saber leading. Asbeel had to cut his swing short and retreat another step.

I kept glancing over my shoulder, expecting the dragon to descend upon us. But the dragon seemed to have disappeared.

With each motion Joen and I were more in tune. My first instinct had been to protect her, to keep myself between the demon and Joen. Though I knew firsthand that she could fight, the thought of Asbeel hurting her made me nauseous. But on the narrow ledge overlooking the dragon's cave, I had no way to stand between them.

And so we fought as one.

The demon rushed forward. I stepped to the side. Then Joen darted in, stabbing at his exposed side. Again and again we repeated the maneuver, until we had turned Asbeel in a full circle.

"I'm done playing with you, children." With murder in his eyes, Asbeel lifted his sword for a final attack.

But another, larger, form rose up behind him.

The bull walrus raised its head and let loose a mighty barking roar. Then it brought its wicked tusks, one broken but the other sharp, down at the demon's back. Asbeel tumbled to the ground.

R.A. & GENO SALVATORE

The demon rolled over quickly, bringing his wicked jagged sword to bear against the walrus. The walrus raised its head and let out another bark. Its sharp tusk glinted in the sunrise.

"Come on," Joen said, grabbing my arm and pulling me. "We've got more important things to do than sit here watching, eh?"

I didn't argue. Off we ran, down the beach to *Sea Sprite* and the two crews. At first Joen led, but soon I had passed her, running so fast with my boots, pulling her along behind. I said a silent thanks to the bull walrus. It wouldn't last long against the likes of Asbeel.

The sun had crested the eastern horizon, and its brilliant light sparkled on the ocean. I looked up to the sky above it. The dragon soared there in a wide arc, exultant in the cold air. It seemed to have lost any concern with us; instead, it swept over the ocean.

"Where do you think he's going?" I asked no one in particular.

"She," Joen responded. "And I think she's headed for the ships. Dragons are smart, you know? Maybe she knows we can't get off the island without a ship."

"Yeah, that makes sense," I said. "We should probably run faster then, don't you think?"

"Oi, sounds like a plan."

The wind went from still to gale in an instant. The new dawn was swept away by the black clouds of an oncoming storm.

We rounded the last bend and saw *Sea Sprite* at the edge of the water. Dozens of sailors scrambled over her, trying to get her into the water. On deck at the stern rail, Captain Deudermont called out his orders. Lightning flashed behind him, casting him in silhouette.

With that captain at the helm, *Sea Sprite* would be ready to go, I knew, and no hail nor gale nor thunder would stop her.

The dragon's wide arc brought it back toward land, making a straight line for the still-beached ship.

The air was suddenly lit, but not by lightning. Out of nowhere, a great ball of fire exploded, high up in the dragon's face.

Its roar took on a deeper timbre, of rage and

agony mingled. It let loose its breath, a blast of electrical energy to rival the storm above.

But its aim was not good, and the thunderstroke hit nothing but the beach, throwing up only sand and stone.

"Nice one, kids," called Robillard, standing calmly at the edge of the camp, casting another fireball as we ran by. "Felt the need to wake a dragon, did you? Not saying I've never had that urge myself, but this really doesn't seem the best time for it."

Joen laughed. "Once in a lifetime opportunity, you know? She was there. How could we pass up the chance?"

"A fair point," Robillard conceded. He muttered an arcane incantation, moved his hands about in some odd gestures, and again a great blast of fire filled the sky, right in the dragon's path.

"And I see you've decided to rile it up even more," I said sarcastically.

"Just making it ready for our friends," he said.

"Friends?"

At the next flash of lightning, Robillard pointed to some smaller shapes flying toward the dragon. Ravens.

"Oi, nice idea!" Joen said.

"Get to the ship already, would you?" Robillard said dryly, and again he fell into spellcasting.

We didn't need to be told twice. The ship had caught a wind-whipped wave and was floating. The crew who had not yet reached the deck were climbing lines.

Suddenly, a wall of fire shot up between us and the ship, cutting across the beach from sea to cliff. I turned behind me. Another fire wall sprang up, blocking our retreat.

Asbeel ambled through the tunnel of fire, looking none the worse for his encounter with the walrus.

"Enough of this," he said. "You will come with me."

Chapter Twenty-Eight

I heard Asbeel's words echoing in the back of my head, compelling me to obey. I strained against them, trying to call up happier times with Perrault, Elbeth, Joen. Anything to get Asbeel's voice out of my mind. But still I found my feet moving, one shuffling step, then another.

"Let him go," Joen said, stepping in front of me, her daggers drawn.

"Let him go," Asbeel repeated in a mocking high-pitched voice.

With a snarl, Joen leaped at him, ignoring the heat of the fiery walls, ignoring that wicked sword, long and curved and jagged and ablaze with demonic red fire.

In a blink, Asbeel's sword was swinging, and Joen was falling away.

My trance broken, I charged at Asbeel with my sword drawn.

Red and blue flame crashed against each other again and again, each contact hissing and throwing off a burst of steam.

Asbeel gave ground willingly, retreating directly toward one of the fire walls. The heat grew as we approached the sheet of flame, and though Asbeel seemed entirely unaffected, I had to halt my advance and fall back.

"Come on then," I snarled, settling into a defensive stance.

"Yeah, bring it, eh?" Joen said, gathering herself up from the ground. I looked at her, stunned. Asbeel's swing had struck her, I was sure of it. But there she was, standing up unhurt, with only a slight tear in her leather tunic.

She saw my look and threw me a wink—all the answer I would get, as the demon was advancing again.

hen Perrault was wounded, I had stood behind
fraid or unable to fight. I would not let that
 again. I would not watch the demon kill
 who fought with me, who fought for me.
reamed as I lunged, throwing my off-balance
 at Asbeel, but at his arm.

aim was true, my sword diving straight for
y forearm. But the demon's arm arm was
—he had released the grip on his sword; his
ve had been a feint. His hand found my
beel spread his wings and jumped, letting
 us.

ll to her back, not hurt, but too far away

silvery glint caught my eye, speeding up
om her prone form. It was one of her
ing through the wind toward its target.
impact as the dagger drove into Asbeel's
his anguished scream. Then suddenly I

r one of the walls of fire.

Joen dropped into a low crouch and moved to her right. I moved to the left. Asbeel shadowed me, moving slowly and deliberately, never exposing more than his side to Joen. He reached out with his sword, a surprisingly tentative strike for such a typically cocky foe. I parried solidly, pushing his sword away.

Again he lunged out lazily, and again I parried. He followed with a quick, shortened horizontal swipe that probably would not have reached me anyway. Still, I tapped the top of his sword with my own and drove the blade down.

I realized my mistake as soon as steel hit steel. He let his blade drop, pulled it down even, and rushed forward. With no resistance, my parry had gone farther than I wanted, and I could not bring my blade to bear. Neither could he, but he had other weapons at his disposal—foremost among them, his own weight.

I tried to step back, but the demon pushed against me, pressing me backward, driving me toward the second wall of fire.

Joen came in hard on his flank, her left dagger up defensively, her right jabbing hard. The demon tried to dodge, but I used my position to my advantage, locking my leg against his, preventing him from taking a step.

Joen's dagger drove into the demon's side. He howled in pain, shoved off me hard, throwing me backward. In a flash, his sword was back in his hand, and he was whipping around. His inhuman strength was on clear display, his sword pummeling through Joen's defenses, sending her tumbling.

My heart dropped, but only for a second. Somehow she came to her feet, apparently unhurt and still holding both daggers.

Asbeel's position had suddenly worsened dramatically. He no longer had a wall of fire to his back; instead he had the two of us on opposite sides, both unhurt.

I moved in, cautiously executing a simple attack routine. Asbeel's sword was there to block each attack, but as Joen moved in from the other side, he had to whip his sword around. Again his strength served him well, and he had the sword around in time, but only just. Joen ducked under his wild swing and fell back.

Which left him defenseless from my side. I lunged in, aiming for a killing blow.

But Asbeel jumped, beating his great black wings once. He was above us, floating over us.

He lashed out with his foot, aiming for my head, but I ducked under the blow.

Joen leaped at him, digg
ankle. The demon howled in
her. She tumbled away. I
had been hit, or had let go
she landed gracefully, rolli
at the ready once more.

The demon beat hi
Joen's head, and droppe

Joen and I met hir
time I attacked, Joen
a perfect complemen
were leading her in a

I swept in from
Joen came in from
jabbing in unison.

Asbeel ducke
sword across to d
Asbeel continue
blades out to t
his sword.

The hilt:
same vicious
before, that
And it

Chapter Twenty-Nine

Waves of heat radiated from the wall as I fell toward it. I grasped at Perrault's cloak, trying in vain to wrap it around me, hoping it would protect me as it had always done. But I could not hold it in the gale.

I closed my eyes. I smelled my hair singeing. I felt my flesh burning. Somewhere I heard Joen scream.

Then the heat was gone. The pain was gone. The scream was gone.

All I heard was the crash of the waves and the howl of the wind.

I opened my eyes and lifted my head from the sand, to find someone standing over me.

"Not satisfied with just a dragon, huh?" Robillard said sarcastically.

"Took you long enough," I heard Joen say, but her words ended in a groan. Asbeel held her aloft, his strong hand around her wrists. Her daggers lay on the ground, both bloody but both useless.

"Release her," Robillard said.

Asbeel laughed. "Come get her."

Robillard said a quick chant and pointed a hand at Asbeel, all five fingers pointing at him. A bolt of red energy leaped from each, darting through the air to burn into Asbeel's flesh.

The demon grimaced briefly, then started laughing again. "The great wizard comes to the rescue, and that's all he can manage?" he said. "What is it, wizard? Are you afraid to harm the girl, or are you just . . . spent?"

Another five bolts leaped at the demon, but again he just laughed.

Overhead, nine ravens circled, descending slowly. *Sea Sprite* drifted away from shore, her sails still furled, waiting for us.

"I think I've worn out my welcome," Asbeel said. "Pity, I was growing quite fond of the worthless rock. Ah, well, I suppose I'll have to take something to remember it by." He beat his wings, catching the wind—which was blowing directly out from the island—and lifted off, still holding Joen by the wrists. "Perhaps you'll come visit me some time, boy?" he chided.

Without thinking, I sprinted down the beach toward him. Loose sand sucked at my feet, yet my pace was ever so fast. I felt a stone beneath my foot, a solid point to push off from.

And I leaped.

An impossible leap, twenty feet into the air, thirty, my sword leading the whole way. Propelled by my magical boots, I caught the demon mid-flight, drove my sword into his flesh just above the hip, into and through. His scream rent the air. He twisted away from me, wrenching Perrault's sword from my grasp.

Down I fell. Joen fell after me, plummeting into the surf thirty feet below.

I plunged into the sea, then emerged choking.

The waves grabbed me, threatening to pull me out to sea, but I paddled furiously and looked up.

Off Asbeel flew, his wings beating awkwardly once, twice, and again. Lightning flashed, and the wings missed a beat. His black form hung in the air for just a moment, then dropped from the sky into the raging seas.

With hardly a sound, my great tormenter disappeared beneath the waves. But it was not without a pang of sadness that I saw him go.

After all, the sword still stuck in his side had served me well.

But then, that sword had only ever had one true mission: to avenge Perrault, its true master. With that accomplished, I supposed, the sword deserved its rest.

A wave washed me up on the shore, depositing me face-first into the sand.

"Nice one, eh," Joen said, spitting seawater and pulling herself up beside me. "Thanks a bunch."

"There'll be time for that later," Robillard said, jogging down the beach to meet us then right out into the surf. "We've got a ship to catch." He held out a hand to each of us. As I took his hand, I shot up to the surface of the water, feeling it hold me as if it were firm ground.

We reached *Sea Sprite* a few minutes later. The storm still raged, but the wind was pushing us away from the island, not trapping us there.

That would be Elbeth's doing, I knew, and I offered a quick thank you to the wind.

CHAPTER THIRTY

Sea Sprite cut through the storm-tossed waters with graceful ease, her tattered sails full of wind, her repaired mast straining but holding fast. For an hour she sailed, putting miles between us and the island, between us and the Circle, and the dragon, and Asbeel.

Joen and I sat huddled in the crow's nest together. It felt an odd sort of homecoming. That place had been so important the first time I'd met her. The gull's nest, she'd called it. But today there were no gulls; the birds we watched for were ravens. And they did not show their faces. Or beaks, as it were.

The sun had not reached halfway into the sky when we broke clear of the storm. Beyond the edge of the storm, the day was bright and clear.

A broad smile stretched across Joen's face. She could not stay seated. She gripped the mast in both hands, letting her weight fall left, then right, a graceful swinging motion. Her arms were bare to the shoulder, revealing several cuts and a few ugly bruises. I sighed deeply and stared at my hands.

"Do you think they'll follow us? Any of them?" she asked, for the fourth time.

"Hope not," I said, resting my head against the side of the crow's nest.

"Me too, eh? Wouldn't be so good to get caught out here, eh?"

"Not good, nope."

"Oi, what is it, then?" she said harshly.

"What is what?"

"This doom and gloom thing you're doing. Didn't you notice, we won?"

"Yeah. Sorry."

"So why so down, eh?"

I looked at her for a long time, studying her face, her forgiving eyes, the smile that had not faded from her features. "I lost my sword, and my cloak is broken," I said.

"Oi, how can you break a cloak?" she said with a laugh.

"Look at it!"

"Already seen it. I think it looks prettier now, anyway. Sorry 'bout the sword, though. Did its job, didn't it, eh?"

"It's more than that. The cloak, the sword, they belonged to Perrault."

"I know," she said as she leaned in. "Just because you lost the sword doesn't mean you lost him. Remember that. He'd be proud of you, don't you think?"

"One of the Circle was someone I knew," I blurted. "Someone I thought was dead."

Joen stopped her swinging and sat down, right beside me, her arm brushing against my own. "The one who whispered to me?"

"Yeah, I think so."

"So she's the one who helped us escape, then? Good thing she was there." She laughed.

"Yeah, definitely. But I just wish . . ." I looked back at my hands. "I don't know."

THE *SHADOWMASK*

"Yes you do. You wish she'd gotten off the island with us. That you would've had more time with her. Right?"

I nodded.

"But aren't you glad to know she isn't dead, at least?"

Again I nodded. I hadn't thought of it like that before.

"And you got the stone, right? Wasn't that the plan?"

"It's also the cause. The stone cost me Perrault, and it cost me his sword, and it's the reason I can't spend more time with Elbeth. It's such a small thing, but it costs me so much."

"It hasn't cost you me," she said, resting her head on my shoulder.

"Yet."

Her head shot back up. "Don't talk like that, eh?" she said sharply.

Below us, on the deck, the two crews worked together with remarkable efficiency. The captain stood at the helm, calling out his orders. The crew moved about, the slow waltz of a seasoned crew, not brothers in arms but brothers in the same goal, their grudges laid aside for a common aim, for a journey home. A fog was rising over the water, over the ship, but Deudermont didn't change course.

I closed my eyes, letting the rhythm of the ocean wash over me.

"Feeling better?" Joen asked, her voice a whisper.

I turned to her, to say yes. But she was so close, too close, not a foot between us. I could feel the heat of her breath, could smell the salt of her hair, could see her half-closed eyes.

The fog crept up into the crow's nest. A part of me wished to pull away, but a much greater part would not, could not.

Her lips were on mine, and all other sensation was gone. All that mattered was the softness of her lips, the—

"Wait," she said, pushing me away.

I blushed. "I'm sorry. I shouldn't have—"

"I know this fog," she cut in, leaning out of the crow's nest. "Listen."

I shook my head. "Listen? For what?" I perked up my ears, trying to focus past the rolling waves and the breeze.

And there it was, unmistakable.

Hoofbeats, familiar hoofbeats, echoed across the water.

Find out how it all ends.

Don't miss the explosive conclusion to the
Stone of Tymora Trilogy, coming *September 2010.*

STONE OF TYMORA · BOOK III

THE SENTINELS

About the Authors

R.A. Salvatore is the author of forty novels and more than a dozen *New York Times* best sellers, including *The Pirate King* which debuted at #3 on *The New York Times* best seller list.

Geno Salvatore has collaborated on several R.A. Salvatore projects including Fast Forward Games' *R.A. Salvatore's The DemonWars Campaign Setting* and *R.A. Salvatore's The DemonWars Player's Guide.* He co-authored R.A. Salvatore's DemonWars *Prologue*, a DemonWars short story that appeared in the comic book published by Devil's Due Publishing. He is a recent graduate of Boston University and lives in Massachusetts.

**Fly through the air with the greatest of ease—
on a silver dragon!**

Jace, a high-wire acrobat in a traveling circus, thought he knew the thrill of adventure. But when he meets Belen, a strange girl with no memory of her past, he soon discovers how much more adventure—and danger—awaits him. Not long after Belen joins the circus, a wizard arrives and stops the show—not by magic, but by accusation. Belen is not human, he says: she is a dragon who destroyed a nearby town. As Jace and Belen set off in a race against time to clear Belen's name and recover her memory, mysterious forces conspire to throw them off track. Can Jace learn to fly through the air with the greatest of ease on the back of a dragon before time runs out? Find out in:

SILVER
DRAGON CODEX